KAALI

VISHAL PUNNA

notionpress.com

INDIA • SINGAPORE • MALAYSIA

Copyright © Vishal Punna 2025
All Rights Reserved.

ISBN
Paperback 979-8-89632-763-9
Hardcase 979-8-89699-403-9

This book has been published with all efforts taken to make the material error-free after the consent of the author. However the author and the publisher do not assume and hereby disclaim any liability to any party for any loss damage or disruption caused by errors or omissions whether such errors or omissions result from negligence accident or any other cause.

While every effort has been made to avoid any mistake or omission this publication is being sold on the condition and understanding that neither the author nor the publishers or printers would be liable in any manner to any person by reason of any mistake or omission in this publication or for any action taken or omitted to be taken or advice rendered or accepted on the basis of this work. For any defect in printing or binding the publishers will be liable only to replace the defective copy by another copy of this work then available.

Contents

Chapter 1

The Dark Awakening

The night felt heavy and suffocating, the shadows pressing in on every side as Rudra stood over David's limp body, his hands slick with blood. His fists throbbed, the skin split from the assault, yet he seemed hardly aware of the pain. He kept his gaze fixed on David, crumpled and lifeless on the cold concrete floor, blood pooling beneath him. Rudra was gasping heavily as if about to burst free, but nothing inside him seemed to calm down.

Silently, behind him, a faint sobbing echoed through the darkness. His head turned sharply, Rudra followed the sound, his footsteps echoing through the empty warehouse. There, chained to the wall, sat Anvi, a small girl with fragile-looking features on tear-streaked cheeks. She couldn't be more than eight, yet she was giving off waves of this terrible fear as she looked up at him, her slight frame overwhelmed by the heavy chain that held her in place, eating away at her wrists. She choked back a sob, her great eyes pleading for help, yet she dared not speak a word.

Without a word, Rudra gathered himself and found his way to her side. He tore at the restraints that held her captive and released them. Anvi's small body slumped with an obvious sense of relief, yet her eyes remained wide and wary. Gingerly, he lifted her into his arms; she was light as a whisper against the bulk of his frame. He held her close like a vice and headed for the door. His goal was nothing more than to get her out of this place.

But a harsh ringing broke the silence. The phone in his pocket buzzed loudly, with the name of an unknown number flashing on the screen. Rudra hardly looked at it and thrust it back into his pocket. And that was it - to be finished with all such interruptions, he thought as he took another step forward. Something inside him twisted then, and the weight of rage rose again, immovable. That wasn't enough. David had been broken and beaten, lying there. But Rudra had to finish with it.

He turned around, his jaw set in a firm line. He put Anvi down gently before reaching for his gun, which had fallen to the floor. The metal felt cold against his palm. Not even for a moment did he think before taking aim at David's limp body, pulling the trigger. The gunshot rang through the warehouse, sealing the space in silence forever. David's body jerked one last time and then lay still. Rudra stood there for a moment, his breath even, his face unreadable. His gaze lingered on David, and only when the echo of the gunshot had faded did, he reach for Anvi once more, holding her close.

Outside, dawn was breaking, casting a grey light over the city. The deserted streets were very silent, punctuated only by a car pulling up to an under-construction building. The vehicle rolled to a stop, its engine cutting off as a figure emerged in a black hoodie. He moved with calculated precision as he walked to the rear of the car and opened the trunk, releasing the sight of the two lifeless bodies inside, positioned like discarded objects. He pulled them out one by one, letting them fall on the gravel. Besides the bodies, he placed a box - a simple, unadorned thing with the word KAALI scribbled in blood.

In the early morning, Khaleel pursued a suspect, his heart racing as they dashed through the winding streets into a half-built structure. The boy dodged and weaved, but Khaleel's drive propelled him forward, with every instinct honed in years of training. He gained on the suspect only to be drawn into a scene that haunted him.

It was dark and quiet in the room, but as soon as Khaleel entered, he saw the two dead bodies stretched on an open-plan concrete floor. A grimness clamped down inside him as his eyes met the box, the ominously labelled one staring back at him... KAALI. He moved slowly towards it like one moving through water. Opening that box confirmed all the worst fears in him. Inside lay the taken-out organs of the victims: the woman's heart and part of the man in a grotesque parody of finality. Khaleel stepped back as bile filled his mouth and throat. He just barely reached the wall to throw up when reality overwhelmed him.

Khaleel wiped his mouth, trying to compose himself. Gathering himself, he picked up his phone to call the police. With great difficulty, he tried explaining the situation to the police in detail. Soon, he could hear sirens approaching the place. It was a blur of a moment for him. Outside, chaos was brewing. Reporters, police, and curious onlookers began to throng around the building, drawn by the whispers of horror. He was soon surrounded by the bright light of dawn, where a crowd of journalists awaited him with microphones and cameras, the questions eager and unrelenting.

Now, one of the reporters shouted to him. "Sir, could you tell us what happened here?" he asked, pushing a microphone towards him.

"We're still investigating," Khaleel rasped out from behind his hands as he squinted to avoid camera lights.

Another voice cut through, one sharper, more insistent. "Is it true that her heart and his genitals were removed, put in the box that had the word 'KAALI' printed on it?"

Khaleel's jaw set in a firm line. "Yes, that's right," he said, his tone clipped.

A new voice cut through the crowd—one that was calm yet piercing. "Sir, Durga from Crime Watch," she pushed her way through to the front of the crowd. Durga, wearing a *kurti* of bright pink and blue jeans, was known for her fearless questioning and sharp investigative instincts. She gave Khaleel a stern stare, notebook ready. "Can you comment on any potential suspects?"

Khaleel nodded, for the weight of the case rested heavily on his shoulders. "No," he said into the receiver, but the strain was clear in his voice, "but we will keep you posted. Thank you."

He sidestepped and pushed to create a path, barely able to fend off the battering of questions as he made his way through the crowd. Durga's eyes never left him; already, her mind was humming with possibilities. She had come for a story, but there was something else here, something sinister and inexplicable that she felt in her bones.

As the sun rose in the morning, tension was rife in the air through rumours that were as contagious as wildfire and burst through the crowd. And whatever lay inside the box marked with KAALI was just beginning to unfold before Durga, and she knew it was just the start of something far darker than what even one could have imagined.

Under the haze of morning light, a milkman pedalled steadily along the narrow lanes. The panniers of his bike were filled with clinking metal cans. The city was just starting to stir, but his thoughts were absorbed in his daily delivery run, moving mentally to the rhythmic task before him. As he approached an underpass, though, he saw something that chilled him. What he saw was unnatural.

Two bodies lay on the sidewalk. Dead, they were a grotesque juxtaposition to the uneventful urban landscape surrounding them. He pressed on the brake reflexively, and the bike skidded to a halt. Pounding in his chest, he stumbled off, accidentally knocking his bike to the pavement. Cold dread, creeping and spreading, struck him; his mind was spinning with panic. His hands were shaking as he reached into his pocket to dial his phone. Shaking and trembling, he dialled 100.

A few minutes passed before Officer Khaleel and his crew arrived, the car crunching over the gravel as they came up to the scene. Yellow tape was quickly drawn around the area, sealing off the gruesome sight from the curious eyes already gathering at a distance. Khaleel stepped out, immediately catching sight of the milkman—pale, jittery, his hands wringing together nervously.

"Tell me what you saw," Khaleel said, his voice steady but with a note of urgency.

The milkman swallowed, his eyes darting nervously between the bodies and the officer. "Sir, I was just on my regular route, delivering milk like usual… then… then I saw them," he stammered, barely above a whisper.

Khaleel followed the man's pointed gesture. The two bodies slumped in unnatural angles, as if carelessly discarded. He knelt down, of course; the familiar markings gleamed in the dim light, his face growing darker moment by moment. A small box lay beside them, smeared with thick congealed blood. The word "KAALI" was written on it in letters that seemed both distorted and sinister. Certainly, the work of one and the same killer - a twisted signature left, taunting or warning.

Khaleel turned to his assistant. "Looks like the same killer has committed this crime," he said, his tone hard.

The assistant nodded warily as he scoured the scene, his eyes scanning everything around him. He, too, understood the implications of what they saw—another chilling message from a predator growing bolder with every passing day.

Meanwhile, on the far end of town, a dusty wasteland dump yard served as a meagre welcome mat to the forgotten. Amidst the rusty jumble of discards that awaited him there, the grizzled man in his forties caught his eye on a dark stain soaking through a torn bag. He swallowed hard when he discovered something horrific; with each step closer, the frown lines on his head increased. Trembling, he backed away, his hand, as if of its own accord, reaching for the phone to ring the police.

Once again, Khaleel's team was sent out, their cop car rumbling over the lumpy terrain of the dump yard. The scene was creepy and silent, with only the hum of machinery in the distance and the low, sad caw of a crow perched nearby. Khaleel stepped out of the vehicle, his face set as he gazed at the bleak surroundings. A man waited by a rusted container, a look of sheer terror on his face.

Khaleel stalked towards him, crunching boots over the littered ground. "Are you the one who called?"

He nodded quickly. "Yeah, I'm the one... Please, just follow me. It's just over there."

"Move out," Khaleel said, motioning forward with a hand. The man led them through a maze of discarded appliances and twisted metal. Each step brought them deeper into the yard, the stench of rot filling the air. Khaleel kept a wary eye on the man as he navigated the treacherous path, ready for anything.

"What exactly did you find?" he asked, his tone calm yet probing.

The man's voice quavered as he explained. "I was scavenging through the scrap metal piles to decide what to sell. That's when I found it. I called you guys right away."

Khaleel narrowed his eyes slightly. "Did you touch anything?"

"No, sir. I didn't touch anything.".

He led them into a secluded corner partially shielded by towering piles of junk. And there, amongst the twisted remnants of discarded lives, lay more bodies. Khaleel's breath hitched slightly as his gaze hardened, taking in the macabre sight before him. The officers exchanged tense glances, visibly affected by the grisly scene.

Like the first two, the bodies stank of the same gruesome omens: an awful rite of violence. And once again, next to the body, a box sat there, it seemed, half intentionally placed, filled with black, thick blood. "KAALI" was splattered over it. The scarlet letters seemed to sneer at them in their ferocity, almost. It was a ritual that appeared so well planned to catch them off balance, to frighten—a haunting notice from a faceless fiend lurking in the city's dark.

Khaleel watched carefully, considering every possible angle and shot. His pulse raced with a tinge of urgency, but he kept himself under control and calm, with focus. Whoever this was, they were cool and calculated and knew how to leave a message both haunting and taunting.

Steel to the task, he turned his entire team around. "Start gathering all the evidence. Nothing is leaving this scene unexamined."

They nodded, leaping to their feet and carefully listing every awful aspect, every shred of tattered evidence. But Khaleel's mind was already racing forward from that moment.

The dim room lay silent as Rudra, a rugged man in his forties, jolted awake, heart pounding, breaths ragged. Sweat beaded on his forehead, the echoes of a nightmare still gripping him. Suddenly, his phone rang, slicing through the silence. He reached for it with trembling hands, an uneasy tension tightening in his chest. As he listened, his face softened, a shadow of sorrow settling over him. The memory struck hard—a haunting vision of Nandini, his love, gasping her final breath, her life slipping away as he stood helpless. The anguish of that moment weighed heavily, raw and unrelenting.

When Anvi stepped out of the jeep, she turned back and waved goodbye to Rudra with her small hand—a bright, cheerful wave. Rudra waved back, a contented smile softening his otherwise rugged face. A buzz from his phone snapped him out of the moment. He glanced at the screen before answering.

"On my way, Sir," he said, his voice transforming from the soft warmth of a father to the steady concentration of a police officer. The line cut off as he started the jeep again and drove away from the school gate, the smile lingering as he replayed Anvi's face before him.

Rudra's jeep finally came in front of the Police Commissioner's office. He manoeuvred it through the gate and smoothly parked it in front of the building. He switched off the engine, came out himself, and gazed with a nearly nostalgic routine at the familiar surroundings.

Head Constable Ali was sitting on a bench just outside. When he saw Rudra step out, he deliberately excused himself from the lively discussion he was having with another officer and strode over. His air changed from casual to respect filled as he approached Rudra.

"How do you do, sir? Behold, so long," Ali greeted with a very easy smile.

He put his hand on Ali's shoulder and smiled at him, "All is well," he said steadily as his voice broke into Ali's train of thought. They walked together towards the Commissioner's room.

Ali glanced at him with a touch of concern passing through his otherwise composed face. "How is Anvi?"

Rudra's face softened. "She's better now," he whispered.

Ali looked down, wringing his hands in sympathy. "Feel so sorry for the girl. Lost her mother at such a young age."

Rudra's jaw tightened ever so slightly, but he nodded in appreciation of Ali's words. They came to the door of the Commissioner's office, and Ali nodded to Rudra before hurrying off.

Rudra waited, then knocked.

Inside, Commissioner Krishna Reddy, a man in his sixties with greying hair and reading glasses perched on his nose, was studying paperwork when he heard the knock. "Come in," he muttered without looking up.

He entered, and as the door clicked shut behind him, Commissioner Reddy looked up and immediately broke into a welcoming smile as he rose from behind his large, polished desk.

"Good to see you, Rudra," he said warmly, extending his hand.

Rudra stepped forward and shook his hand firmly. "Good to see you too, sir," he replied.

They both sat down now, and the atmosphere shifted a little from personal to professional as they settled in.

Rudra, ever direct, leaned forward, his eyes unyielding on the Commissioner. "Sir, why did you call me?"

The Commissioner's smile never wavered, but there was something paternal in the way he regarded him. "First, tell me—how's Anvi?"

Taking a deep breath, Rudra looked into Krishna Reddy's unwavering eyes. "She's alright now," he said softly, his lips curling up faintly with a trace of a smile at the mention of Anvi's name.

The Commissioner leaned back in his chair, his eyes acutely perceptive and sharp. "The reason I called you in, Rudra," he said, "is that I need you to take up a case." Pausing for a glance at Rudra, he went on, "I'm sure you must have heard about the recent killings in the city. It's getting out of hand, and I want you to take over."

Rudra's face turned dark. He had heard of the killings, a series of brutal murders of no apparent connection to one another that left an arc of shadow over the city. He shook his head sharply, and the memories of the past clenched his heart in a vice. "I know about the murders, Sir, and you know it's impossible. I quit this job after. After what happened to Nandini. Now I have Anvi to look after."

Reddy's eyes softened, but his voice didn't waver. "I know, Rudra, but for how long will you keep blaming yourself for her?"

"As long as it takes," he said, his voice quiet but filled with unyielding force. The weight of Nandini's death, his failure to protect her, was a burden he couldn't shake off; one he did not want to shake off.

The Commissioner leaned forward. He altered his tone to almost pleading. "Rudra, please understand. We need you on this case. It's a personal request. Please. Think about it."

Unspoken memories and unshed tears hung heavily in the air, yet silence hung between them. Finally, Rudra stood up, his face still unreadable. He extended his hand, and the Commissioner took it, though he could feel Rudra's reluctance.

He bowed gently and stepped out of the office as if sealing the issue. But, as he opened the door to his jeep, he was not at peace.

He opened the creaky door of his jeep to see Constable Ali standing by it. His face had a mixture of curiosity and concern. "Sir, why were you called in?" he asked, unable to hide his curiosity.

Rudra's jaw worked in contemplation before he looked away, lost in thought. "He wants me to take up the recent killing case," he said, his voice low and somewhat mean, as if saying it aloud made it harder to bear.

Ali's eyes widened, but that was no surprise. "What did you tell him?"

"I told him I can't," Rudra said curtly. His eyes spoke more than his words ever could.

But then Ali's expression softened, and he stepped closer to him, saying, lowering his voice, "Sir, please. Think about it again. These killings are brutal, and my nephew, Khaleel, is in charge now. If he could work under you, he'd learn a lot. Please consider that."

Rudra glanced at Ali, the plea in his old friend's eyes striking a chord in his chest. As he started the jeep and merged into the city's churning traffic, his mind was a storm of conflicting emotions.

Night had fallen when Rudra sat alone in his living room, filled only by the soft hum of the fan, the air thick and silent. He sat forward on the couch, his head bowed, fingers rubbing his forehead to quiet down the turmoil welling up inside him—the case, Nandini, that unyielding grief he carried.

Nandini's mother had approached him in silence, placing a gentle hand on his shoulder. He knew that was her silent comfort, the warmth he'd come to depend on. She sat beside him, steady as the anchor he often needed.

"What happened?" she asked. "What are you thinking about so much?"

Rudra let out a deep sigh and looked down. His voice was subdued. "Nothing, Ma."

She looked at him kindly, a 'come on, you can tell me' look. "You know you can tell me, right?"

He nodded after a beat and resigned. "The Commissioner called me into the office today," he began slowly, the words measured as if he stepped on each one before pronouncing them. He wants me to take over a case."

Her eyebrows rose a fraction. "So, what is there to think about? If he's asking you to work on it, it must be an important one."

Rudra shook his head. "It is... but that's not the point." His voice dropped to a near whisper. "We lost Nandini during the last case I worked on. I can't let anything happen to you or Anvi."

Nandini's mother's face smoothed; a gentle hand reached out and closed over his own. She squeezed it lightly, her voice a balm to his exhausted heart. "Why are you expecting something bad will happen? And about Nandini... it was never your fault."

The words seemed a gentle prod to a locked door in Rudra's heart, one he had not yet prepared to open. But as he looked into Nandini's mother's eyes, all he could feel was an understanding that seemed bottomless, full of love that never wavered, no matter how lost he had felt.

She went on, her voice firm yet tender. "If you ask me, I want you to work on this case. Think of the people who have lost their loved ones due to this killer. Even they must have families... children, like Anvi."

Rudra remained silent, his mind reeling. The reality was, he had never really thought of the victims - those bereaved families left by the violence. He had been too immersed in himself, his own pain, his own guilt. But now, Nandini's mother's words brought to light a rather different perspective and a sense of duty he just could not ignore.

Finally, he looked up, his voice a mere whisper. "I will think about it, Ma."

She smiled, patted his hand, and stood up, leaving him alone with his thoughts. She knew he needed time to come to terms with his decision.

And so, as the house finally quieted in silence, Rudra's mind went again to the Commissioner's words, Ali's pleading gaze, and now to Nandini's mother's soft nudge. He closed his eyes and saw Nandini's face before him - she had smiled at him with such an intense smile, and laughter filled his life; how could he bring her back to him? He couldn't, but perhaps, in small ways, he could do what he knew best - protect others.

And so, in the first gleams of dawn pouring into the room, Rudra felt a resolve he had lacked. His heart was steady now, and he rose, the weight of his grief somehow lighter, softened by a sense of purpose he felt again.

It was time to face the darkness again. But this time, he would not run from it. This time, he'd face it head-on. For Nandini. For Anvi. For the families waiting for answers. And for the memory of a love that still gives him strength even in the face of his deepest fears.

Chapter 2

The Weight of Responsibility

Rudra sat alone on his couch, the dim light of the living room casting long shadows around him. He was deep in thought, his mind tangled in a web of contemplation that seemed to have no clear end. After a moment, he exhaled a deep breath, as if trying to release the weight of his thoughts and reached out for his phone perched on the coffee table in front of him. His fingers hovered over the screen, hesitating for the briefest of moments before he dialled a number. With a resolute motion, he brought the phone to his ear.

The scene shifted to the quiet bedroom of the Commissioner, who was blissfully asleep under the gentle hum of the night. His phone lay resting on the bedside table, an unnoticed sentinel until it suddenly erupted in sound, shattering the stillness. The Commissioner stirred, reaching out with a groggy hand to grasp the phone. The screen's bright light momentarily blinded him, causing him to squint as he answered the call.

"Yes, this is the Commissioner," he mumbled, his voice thick with sleep.

Back in his apartment, Rudra straightened up, his voice firm and unwavering as he spoke into the phone. "Sir, I am willing to take up the case, but there is one condition."

The Commissioner, now more alert, replied with a hint of curiosity. "Tell me, Rudra."

Rudra paused, ensuring his words were clear and understood. "Sir, as you are aware, I prefer to work on cases without any interference. If you can agree to that, I will take on the case."

There was a moment of silence as the Commissioner considered the request. Finally, he agreed, his voice carrying the weight of authority. "You have my permission, Rudra."

A sense of relief washed over Rudra. "Thank you, sir," he said, his tone filled with gratitude and resolve.

Without wasting any time, Rudra quickly dialled another number. The line connected, and a familiar voice answered, "Ali here, Sir."

"Ali," Rudra began, his voice steady, "I understand your nephew is currently working on the case?"

"Yes, sir," came the reply from Constable Ali, his voice respectful and attentive.

"Please inform him to meet me tomorrow at the station around ten in the morning with all the details related to the case," Rudra instructed, his mind already racing with ideas and strategies.

The conversation ended. Rudra's thoughts were now charged with purpose and determination as the room settled back into a hushed quiet.

The room was sparse but functional, with its dim lighting casting long shadows across the walls. Khaleel and Ali sat side by side at a small desk, a faint air of tension lingering between them as they waited. The sound of a door creaking open broke the silence, and both men instinctively straightened in their chairs as Rudra entered.

Rudra's presence filled the room immediately – a tall figure with an authoritative air, his expression calm yet intense. His dark eyes swept across the room, taking in every detail as though already piecing together unseen puzzles. He moved purposefully to the desk, his polished shoes making a soft clicking sound on the tiled floor.

Khaleel and Ali quickly got to their feet, their movements sharp and practiced. Both raised their hands in a crisp salute.

"Good morning, sir!" they said in unison, their voices steady but edged with respect.

Rudra returned their salute with a curt nod, his lips barely moving as he responded, "Good morning."

Ali stepped forward; his uniform slightly creased but his demeanour eager to please. "Sir, this is my nephew, Khaleel," he said, gesturing towards the younger man beside him. "He's the officer in charge of this case."

Rudra's gaze shifted to Khaleel, studying him for a moment. Khaleel was young but carried himself with a certain confidence, though it was clear he wasn't immune to the pressure of Rudra's scrutiny.

"Khaleel," Rudra began, his voice low and commanding, "your uncle mentioned you were the first officer to arrive at the crime scene. I need you to walk me through what you saw. Leave nothing out, no matter how insignificant it might seem. And tell me—did you find any clues?"

Khaleel reached for a folder resting on the desk, his movements deliberate, as though the weight of the contents had seeped into his very demeanour. He picked it up and handed it over to Rudra with a measured gesture. The folder, plain and unassuming on the outside, held a grim reality within.

Rudra accepted it without a word, his jaw tightening slightly as he flipped it open. His sharp eyes scanned the images inside, each photograph painting a vivid and horrifying picture of the crime scene. The silence in the room thickened as he examined them, and the severity of the violence was evident in every detail captured.

The pictures revealed chaos frozen in time. Blood streaked the floor in jagged lines, pooling around the lifeless forms of the victims. One photograph showed a wooden box, its contents macabre and almost unimaginable—clear signs of cruelty and twisted intent. Rudra's brows furrowed deeply as he processed the visual onslaught, his mind beginning to piece together the fragmented story of what had transpired.

Khaleel and Ali watched him intently from the sidelines, their anticipation palpable. Khaleel's lips parted as if to speak, and finally, he broke the oppressive silence.

"The man's penis and the woman's heart," Khaleel said, his voice low and grim, "were kept inside the box. The word *'KAALI'* was written on it."

Rudra didn't lift his gaze from the photographs, his expression unreadable as he absorbed the gruesome revelation. His silence was not dismissive but purposeful, as though he was carefully cataloguing each detail in his mind.

Khaleel, unable to hold back his disgust, muttered, "How can someone be so cruel?"

Rudra finally spoke, his voice measured and steady despite the horror of what he was discussing. "Did you find out anything about the victims? Who are they, or what do they do?"

Khaleel shifted on his feet, his discomfort evident as he began to explain. "Sir, one of the victims was a prostitute. She even had a son, just five years old. But the other woman... she was a housewife. She had an eight-year-old daughter."

Rudra's gaze sharpened at the mention of the children, and he leaned back slightly, the weight of the information pressing down on him. "So," he said, his tone thoughtful, "the killer is targeting women with young children. But why?"

As if speaking the question aloud would somehow provide clarity, Rudra glanced back at the photos before continuing. "Did you talk to or meet any family members?"

Khaleel nodded but hesitated before replying. "The prostitute doesn't have any family. The man who was found next to her... he's a truck driver. He only comes to the area when he has work. There's no permanent connection."

Rudra's expression darkened further. "And what about the housewife? The woman with the eight-year-old daughter?"

"I informed her husband," Khaleel replied, his tone tinged with empathy. "He was out of town at the time. He said he'd be returning today."

Rudra closed the folder with a sharp snap, his movements brisk and purposeful. He strode towards the board mounted on the wall, where a clean space waited. Without hesitation, he pinned the crime scene photographs in a neat yet jarring display, each image now part of a larger puzzle.

He stood back and stared at the board, the harsh lighting casting shadows across his face. "This is a vendetta," Rudra said, his voice firm and tinged with grim certainty. "He's not just killing them. He's making them endure hell before they die."

Turning away from the board, Rudra's gaze met Khaleel's. His eyes, now brimming with resolve, seemed to pierce through the younger officer's uncertainty. The room fell silent again, the weight of Rudra's words lingering in the air like an unspoken vow.

Rudra's tone was sharp and direct as he turned his gaze back to Khaleel. "What does forensics have to say about this?" he asked, his words slicing through the tense silence like a blade.

Khaleel hesitated for a brief moment before replying, "We are still waiting for their report, sir." His voice was steady, though the weight of the case seemed to press down on him visibly.

Rudra's expression remained unreadable, but his displeasure was evident in the clipped way he asked his next question. "Who's handling the forensics?"

"Dr. Srikanth," Khaleel answered promptly, straightening slightly as he spoke the name.

"Call him," Rudra instructed without missing a beat. "Let him know we'll be coming over to meet him shortly."

Khaleel nodded, his movements swift as he retrieved his phone from his pocket. Stepping aside to a quieter corner of the room, he dialled the number, his voice low as he conveyed the message to Dr. Srikanth.

Meanwhile, Rudra's attention shifted back to the board where the crime scene photographs were now pinned. He stood before it, his tall frame casting a shadow over the grim images as he scanned them methodically. His sharp eyes darted from one photo to another, searching for patterns, connections, or clues that might have slipped through the cracks during the initial investigation.

The photos, taken from various angles, revealed every grisly detail of the scene. Blood spatter patterns painted the walls and floors, each marking a macabre story frozen in time. The wooden box, grotesquely central to the scene, seemed to mock its viewers with its horrific contents. Rudra's eyes narrowed as he analysed the evidence, his mind working at lightning speed to piece together the fragmented narrative.

"Also," Rudra said, his voice breaking the silence but still focused on the images before him, "call the victim's husband. I want to hear what he has to say."

Khaleel, now finishing his call with Dr. Srikanth, acknowledged Rudra's command with a quick nod. He ended the call and returned to Rudra's side, a sense of urgency in his stride.

"Sir," Khaleel said, his tone firm and efficient, "we can meet him now."

Rudra's eyes lingered on the board for a moment longer. Then, with a sharp motion, he grabbed his phone from the table, his every action deliberate and purposeful. "Let's go," he said, his tone leaving no room for delay.

Durga had been sitting quietly inside the police station, her gaze fixed on the door, anticipation etched on her face. The moment she spotted Khaleel walking out with Rudra and Ali, she stood up abruptly. Her posture was stiff, determination radiating from her as she made her way towards them.

"Khaleel Sir, I need to talk to you," she called out, her voice steady despite the evident tension beneath.

The trio was already moving purposefully, their strides unbroken. At the sound of her voice, Khaleel turned, his brows knitting together in mild confusion. He came to a halt, his body language a mix of weariness and guarded curiosity.

"Who are you?" Khaleel asked, his tone clipped and direct.

Durga stopped a few paces away, her hands clasped tightly in front of her. "Sir, I am Durga. We met at the crime scene a few days ago."

Recognition flickered briefly in Khaleel's eyes, but he gave a non-committal nod and turned away, resuming his stride. His disinterest was palpable. Without hesitation, Durga hurried after him, refusing to be dismissed so easily.

The group stepped outside into the harsh glare of the afternoon sun. The air outside the station was heavy, a stark contrast to the controlled tension within. The distant hum of traffic blended with the murmurs of passers-by, but Durga's focus remained solely on Khaleel.

"Sorry, I don't have any information for you," Khaleel said curtly, his voice tinged with finality. He moved towards the police jeep, the faint sound of gravel crunching beneath his boots as he approached the vehicle.

Durga followed him, her persistence unwavering. "Sir, any information would help," she implored, her voice carrying a quiet desperation.

Khaleel opened the driver's side door and slid into the seat with practiced ease. He cast a quick glance toward Rudra and Ali, who were already seated inside the vehicle, their expressions neutral but observant.

The exchange seemed routine to them, another fragment of the day's endless inquiries.

Durga stood by the jeep, her stance resolute despite Khaleel's dismissive demeanour. Her plea lingered in the air, the weight of her words pressing against the indifference she faced. For a moment, it seemed as though Khaleel might reconsider. But then, with a slight shake of his head, he gripped the steering wheel, ready to drive away.

The air inside the car was thick with unspoken tension. Khaleel gripped the steering wheel firmly, his knuckles whitening as he manoeuvred the vehicle out of the station's lot. The faint hum of the engine filled the cabin, broken only by the sound of gravel crunching beneath the tyres.

"Sorry, as of now, I don't have any information," Khaleel said, his voice low and firm, though there was a hint of impatience lacing his words.

Through the rearview mirror, Durga's figure remained visible, standing still as she watched the car retreat. Her expression, a mixture of frustration and disappointment, lingered in Rudra's mind as he caught one last glance at her through the side mirror.

Their eyes had met, just briefly, before he turned away. The silent exchange was enough to leave a faint impression.

With a slight adjustment, Khaleel reversed the car and then turned it around smoothly. The station shrank in the distance until it disappeared entirely.

Inside the vehicle, a tense quite persisted. Rudra shifted slightly in his seat; his brow furrowed in thought as he broke the silence.

"Who's she?" Rudra asked, his tone measured. "And why is she so interested in the case?"

Khaleel exhaled sharply, keeping his eyes on the road. "She said her name is Durga. She's a crime reporter."

Rudra nodded slowly, absorbing the information.

"She's looking for information about the case," Khaleel added, his voice carrying a faint undertone of annoyance.

Rudra leaned back in his seat, his fingers drumming lightly on the armrest. "Let's focus on getting information from the doctor first. Then we'll decide how to deal with her."

From the backseat, Constable Ali, who had been quietly studying the crime scene photographs, spoke up. "Sir, looking at these pictures… it looks personal. Why would someone cut off their private parts and kill them?"

Rudra turned his head slightly towards Ali, his sharp gaze thoughtful. "Ali, maybe you're right. But we can't jump to conclusions just yet. We need evidence, not guesses."

Ali nodded, though his gaze lingered on the grim images in his hands, the brutality etched into his mind.

As the car weaved through the bustling streets, the hospital loomed ahead, its stark, white structure a stark contrast to the chaos of the case they were unravelling.

The fluorescent lights of the hospital corridor cast a harsh glow, making the pristine walls appear almost sterile. The faint smell of antiseptic hung in the air, mingling with the muffled sounds of distant conversations and the occasional beep of medical equipment.

Rudra and Khaleel strode purposefully down the corridor, their polished shoes clicking against the tiled floor. Behind them, Ali followed closely, the tension evident in every step.

As they approached a door labelled "Forensic Department," Khaleel reached out, his fingers brushing against the cold metal handle. He pushed the door open, stepping aside to let Rudra and Ali enter first.

The door closed softly behind them, sealing them in the room where more answers—and perhaps more questions—awaited.

The morgue room was cold, the air heavy with the faint smell of formaldehyde. The fluorescent lights overhead cast a stark, pale glow, illuminating every corner of the space. Dr. Srikanth, a man in his sixties with silver hair that matched his wire-rimmed glasses, sat at his cluttered desk. Stacks of papers and thick case files were spread out before him, creating a fortress of information. He meticulously sifted through the documents, pausing occasionally to jot down notes in a spidery scrawl.

Khaleel led Rudra and Ali into the room, their presence breaking the monotonous silence.

"Hello, Dr.," Khaleel greeted warmly, his voice cutting through the quiet.

Dr Srikanth looked up from his work, his eyes tired but sharp. "Hi, Khaleel," he replied with a faint smile, pushing his glasses further up his nose.

"Dr., this is Officer Rudra," Khaleel said, gesturing towards the tall, imposing figure standing beside him. "He is going to lead the investigation."

Rudra stepped forward, extending a polite nod. "Dr, I would like to see the bodies," he said, his tone steady and authoritative.

Dr. Srikanth rose from his chair, his movements deliberate, as though weighed down by years of experience and the burden of his work. "Follow me," he said, leading the way across the room to the cold storage cabinets that housed the deceased.

As they walked, Dr. Srikanth glanced over his shoulder, his expression sombre. "Rudra, I can tell you one thing," he began, his voice carrying a gravity that hinted at the complexity of the case. "This is not the usual murder case."

Rudra exchanged a brief look with Khaleel, his jaw tightening.

Dr Srikanth reached the row of storage cabinets and unlocked the first one with a practiced hand. The heavy metallic clink of the lock echoed in the room as he slid the door open. The body inside lay motionless, its pallor stark against the sterile white sheet. One by one, he opened the cabinets, revealing the grim remnants of lives cut short.

"In my thirty years of work," Dr. Srikanth continued, his voice tinged with a mix of astonishment and weariness, "I have not seen anything like this before."

Rudra stepped closer; his sharp gaze fixed on the bodies as though trying to glean answers from the stillness. "I'm hoping you have some answers now, Doctor," he said, his voice steady but expectant.

Dr Srikanth sighed deeply, his shoulders sagging slightly. "Sometimes, even I am left with more questions than answers," he admitted, his tone reflective. "But please, give me some more time. I'll update you as soon as I have something concrete."

Rudra nodded; his expression unreadable. "Sure, Dr," he replied simply.

Dr. Srikanth closed the cabinet doors with a soft thud, his movements careful and deliberate. Turning back to Rudra, he regarded him with a faint air of caution. "Rudra," he said, his voice taking on a note of quiet seriousness, "Remember, sometimes the truth isn't what we expect it to be."

Rudra held the doctor's gaze for a moment, his sharp eyes reflecting both determination and the weight of what lay ahead. The silence in the room deepened, a solemn reminder of the mysteries they had yet to unravel.

The sterile atmosphere of the morgue pressed down on everyone present, thick with the weight of loss and unanswered questions. The sound of hurried footsteps broke the silence, and all eyes turned toward the man who had just entered. His face was pale, his expression one of dread. Officer Khaleel stepped forward; his voice steady but probing.

"Are you Sashi?" he asked, his gaze fixed on the man.

"Yes, I am," Sashi replied, his voice trembling, barely audible.

Sashi's eyes drifted past Khaleel to the body lying on the cold steel slab. His breath caught in his throat as the reality of the scene hit him. He took a shaky step forward, his body seemingly moving on instinct. His trembling hands reached out, brushing against the lifeless cheek of his wife. Her skin was icy, a cruel confirmation of her absence.

"Priya..." he whispered, his voice cracking under the weight of his anguish. Tears streamed down his face as he stood there, frozen in a moment that felt like an eternity.

Rudra, watching from the side, waited for a few moments before stepping forward. His tone was measured, careful, yet unyielding. "I am sorry for your loss, but you will have to come to the station for questioning."

Sashi didn't respond. His shoulders sagged; his body wracked with silent sobs. Without looking at anyone, he turned abruptly and stumbled out of the room, his movements erratic as though his legs could barely carry him.

He moved through the hospital corridors in a daze, barely aware of his surroundings. The familiar buzz of activity—the clatter of carts, the hurried footsteps of nurses, the soft hum of machines—was nothing but a distant murmur to him. People stepped aside as he passed, their concerned glances following his dishevelled figure, but he didn't notice them. His mind was elsewhere, consumed by the haunting image of Priya lying cold and lifeless in the morgue.

The automatic glass doors at the hospital's exit slid open as Sashi stepped outside, the warmth of the sun hitting him in stark contrast to the chill in his heart. He staggered across the parking lot, his feet dragging as if weighed down by invisible chains.

Reaching his car, he fumbled with the door handle, his shaking hands finally managing to open it. He climbed into the driver's seat and slammed the door shut behind him. For a moment, he sat still, his hands gripping the steering wheel tightly. Then, with a guttural cry, he pounded his fists against the wheel, the sound reverberating sharply in the confined space.

His chest heaved as he gasped for air, his grief threatening to consume him. Blinking through his tears, he looked up and caught sight of something through the windscreen.

Officer Rudra stood at the hospital entrance, watching him intently. His expression was unreadable, his posture still. Yet there was something in his gaze—sharp, unwavering—that Sashi couldn't ignore.

For a long moment, Sashi stared back, the weight of Rudra's presence pressing on him like an unspoken accusation. Then, without a word, he turned his head away, his thoughts swirling with confusion, fear, and an unbearable sense of loss.

Chapter 3

Bonds of the Past and Present

The orphanage stood bathed in the golden sunlight of the late morning, its modest walls radiating warmth. The sound of children's laughter floated through the air, blending seamlessly with the rustling of leaves in the garden. Rudra exited his car, accompanied by Nandini's mother and her young daughter, Anvi. In his hand, he held a neatly folded cheque, a gesture of charity in memory of Nandini.

As Rudra reached the entrance, his eyes were caught by the courtyard. The place was a sea of playful children, so he did not notice Durga immediately. But then he saw her standing in the centre of the garden amidst a flock of kids. Her laughter rose out clear and catchy as she knelt at their level, talking with gesticulations. She looked perfectly carefree, her casual air combining well with the innocence of the children around her. Durga, mid-laugh, suddenly caught sight of Rudra standing by the gate. Her expression altered as recognition was suddenly ignited on her face. Spurning a quick word to the children, she stood up and headed towards him. Her steps were hurried yet at the same time elegant.

"Hello, sir," she said warmly, her voice still tinged with excitement.

Rudra nodded politely, a faint smile on his face. "Hi."

"I am Durga," she said, not at all discouraged. "I am a reporter. We met the other day at the station."

"Yes, I remember," Rudra replied, his tone neutral but not unkind.

Before the conversation could continue, the warden of the orphanage approached them. A kindly man with a gentle demeanour, he extended his hand in greeting. "Hello, Sir and Madam," he said with a respectful bow of his head. "I've been waiting for you."

Rudra shook his head. "Hello, Sir," he replied, his voice steady.

The warden turned his eyes to Anvi and placed a reassuring hand on her head. Initially shy, Anvi looked up at him and was then distracted by the ruckus in the garden. Her eyes welled up as she caught a glimpse of children playing tag. Something sparkled inside her, and she took off running towards them without any caution, little feet scuffling in gravel as she joined the game.

Her laughter soon grew to intertwine with the other kids', forming a symphony of happiness that filled the air. She sprang between her new friends, her face radiant with pure, unfiltered happiness.

Rudra sat at a distance to watch her, his face now softening in a symphony of emotions: pride, longing, and bittersweet ache. Nandini would have loved this moment, he thought. She would have loved to see Anvi so carefree, her laughter echoing through the garden like a song.

Nandini's mother stood beside him, her presence quiet but reassuring. She placed a hand on his shoulder, her touch a silent gesture of support as they both observed Anvi's delight.

Nearby, Durga stood watching too, her eyes reflecting the quiet warmth of the scene. Though she didn't speak, her expression conveyed an unspoken understanding of the emotions unfolding before her.

The warden watched in quiet satisfaction too. Hands clasped behind his back, he nodded to himself, pleased to see Anvi integrating so effortlessly, her joy spreading like a ripple through the group of children.

The moment felt timeless, as if the weight of grief and the simplicity of joy had found a fragile, beautiful balance in the garden that day.

The orphanage grounds warmed with the orange hue of the afternoon sun, and children's laughter filled the air. The warden's face radiated satisfaction as he watched Anvi play with the others; her guffaws blended so well with theirs. He turned around to Rudra with a beaming grin.

"I am so happy to see Anvi like this," the warden said, his voice gentle and sincere. "Please try to bring her more often. It's good for her."

Rudra nodded, his expression softening. "I will," he promised, a quiet determination in his tone.

Rudra reached into his pocket, pulling out the cheque he had brought with him. He offered it to the warden, who took it gladly, beaming with gratitude.

"Thank you for what you've been doing for the children these past few months," the warden said, his gratitude evident.

Rudra glanced at the children playing in the garden, his gaze lingering on Anvi. "I'm just continuing what Nandini always did," he replied, his voice carrying a mixture of pride and sorrow.

The warden hesitated for a moment before speaking again. "Sir, could you please come inside to sign some papers?"

"Of course," Rudra said, following the warden towards the orphanage building.

As Rudra went inside, Durga and Nandini's mother moved forward to a bench which was somewhat shaded by a tall tree. They sat down looking at Anvi, playing with the other children, her laughter weaving brightly in the still atmosphere. Durga turned to Nandini's mother who seemed to be a little hesitant but curiously asked, "Aunty, if you don't mind, may I ask who Nandini is?"

A soft smile touched the older woman's face, though her eyes betrayed the lingering pain beneath. "Nandini was my daughter," she said simply.

Durga hesitated, choosing her words carefully. "And where is she now?"

The older woman's smile faded, replaced by a quiet sadness. "She passed away a year ago," she said, her voice low but steady.

Durga's face softened at the sympathy. "Aww, I'm so sorry to hear that," she said genuinely. The two said nothing for a while as they listened to her revert to being at the centre of the children's game now. Her joy was contagiously a momentary balm for the shadows of grief trailing around their hearts.

I understand what Anvi is going through after losing her mother at such a tender age," Durga broke the silence, speaking in a lower tone now.

Nandini's mother cast a fleeting glance at her, the fire of curiosity flashing in her eyes.

Durga offered a faint smile. "I, too, lost my parents when I was really little," she admitted, a vulnerability in her voice.

The older woman's hand shot out instinctively, a gesture of comfort. "I'm so sorry for your loss. What do you do, dear?"

"I'm a journalist," Durga said, her voice regaining a measure of strength. "I'm working on the same case as Rudra,"

Before their conversation could continue, Rudra emerged from the orphanage building and walked towards them, his steps purposeful but unhurried.

"Let's go, Maa," he said to his mother, his voice gentle but firm. She nodded, rising from the bench. Durga followed her lead, brushing off the folds of her kurta as she stood. "Are you done with work?" Nandini's mother asked, looking up at him.

"Yes, Mom," Rudra said, a small smile twisting his mouth. He headed towards the garden. "Anvi! Vamucelle!"

Anvi paused from her game, turning to come towards him. She waved excitedly at her new friends and dashed towards Rudra and her grandmother; her face rosy with joy.

As she got near, Rudra took her small hand into his - gentle yet firm - gripped hers and walked along with her toward the car as the laughter of children and the silent hollowness of the orphanage swept across her back.

The children's laughter echoed through the yard as they gathered around Durga, their bright faces filled with excitement. Their small hands tugged at hers, their voices blending into a cheerful chorus as they urged her to join their game. Durga laughed, her smile radiant as she allowed herself to be pulled into their world of play and joy.

"Bye, Sir. Bye, Aunty. Bye, Anvi," she called over her shoulder, her eyes meeting Rudra's for a fleeting moment. There was a spark of understanding in her gaze, a fleeting warmth that lingered as she turned to the children.

Rudra stood still for a moment, watching her with a faint smile before turning to his mother. She was also observing Durga, her expression thoughtful and soft.

"Poor girl," she murmured, her voice low and filled with sympathy. "She lost her parents when she was young too."

Rudra nodded silently; his mind weighed down by the thought. Together, they walked towards the car, the cheerful sound of Anvi's laughter filling the air as she skipped happily beside them, her newfound friends waving goodbye from afar.

Durga, meanwhile, was still surrounded by the children, her laughter blending effortlessly with theirs. She waved at Rudra and his family once more before being drawn completely into the lively energy of the orphanage.

Later, back in her apartment, Durga's movements were rushed and purposeful. The clock on the wall showed she was running late, and every second seemed to pass faster than the last. She grabbed her bag and keys from the table, glancing once at her reflection in the mirror to ensure she was presentable. Just as she reached for the door, her phone rang sharply, cutting through the silence of the room.

The screen displayed her boss's name, *Mohan*. She hesitated, her hand hovering over the handle, before sighing and answering the call. "Sir, I'm on my way. I'll be there as soon as possible," she said quickly, trying to mask her anxiety.

Hanging up, she pulled the door shut behind her and descended the stairs, her mind racing with thoughts of the day ahead.

The parking lot outside her office was crowded, but Durga navigated it with ease, weaving her bike into a narrow space between two larger vehicles. She killed the engine, stepped off, and secured her bike before heading towards the building entrance at a brisk pace. Her phone buzzed again as she approached the elevator.

Fumbling through her bag, she finally found the device and answered, "In the lift, coming," she said, her words hurried but clear. She stepped into the elevator as the doors slid open, pressing the button for her floor and tapping her foot impatiently as it ascended.

The elevator doors opened to reveal the bustling office floor, a sea of cubicles stretching out before her. Durga moved through them with practiced urgency, her presence drawing curious glances from her colleagues as she headed straight for Mohan's cabin. Without pausing, she pushed the door open and stepped inside, ready to face whatever awaited her.

Durga stepped into the boss's cabin; the air inside thick with tension. A man in his mid-sixties and the owner of the news company sat behind a wide desk, his glasses perched on the edge of his nose. His sharp eyes, framed by years of wisdom and authority, locked onto Durga as she entered.

"It seems like you are my boss, not me," said Mohan dryly, his voice a mix of reprimand and wry amusement. Durga stiffened slightly but composed herself in no time. "Sorry, sir," she said respectfully yet firmly.

Mohan leaned back in his chair, his fingers steepled as he scrutinised her. "I have been reviewing the progress of the case you are handling. Not a single breakthrough, and we are all worried." Durga nodded, a hint of frustration on her face that was quickly masked. "I understand, sir. I am pushing everything possible to work it forward.

"This case is a priority one," Mohan said, his voice now stern. "We need results, not just attempts."

"I'm very well aware of its importance," Durga replied, her tone resolute. "I've been working extra hours, following every lead I could find."

Mohan studied her for a moment, his expression softening slightly. "I appreciate your efforts, Durga. But effort isn't enough. We need tangible outcomes. What's your plan moving forward?"

Durga hesitated for the briefest moment before responding. "Officer Rudra Pratap has taken over the case, sir. I'm working to collaborate with him to gather more information and make faster progress."

"Rudra Pratap?" Mohan's brows lifted in recognition. "You mean the same Rudra Pratap who made headlines across India a year ago?"

"Yes, sir," Durga confirmed. "How do you know him?"

Mohan's voice sounds reflective now. "A year ago, he was leading a case that stunned the entire nation with its complexity. He pushed himself through every step of it to prove himself, making his unyielding strength more invaluable than any material advantage in the world. And all that while, he lost Nandini."

Durga's face softens. "Yes, I know. I met Rudra and Nandini's mother at an orphanage recently. She mentioned it offhand."

And with that, though at first, she hesitated, her voice took a sharp, determined tone. "Sir, if it's not too much trouble, do talk to him. Maybe you could persuade him to let me join his team. I really think it would help the investigation."

Mohan looked at her, thoughts ticking away as he tapped his fingers lightly on the desk. "You want me to intervene and speak to Rudra?"

"Yes, sir," said Durga. "Please, sir. I'm sure it would make a difference. He's not the most approachable person, but I think together, we could make significant progress."

Mohan let out a sigh and leaned forward. "Alright, I'll talk to him. But if he agrees, make sure you stick to him. Rudra is one of the best. If anyone can crack this case, it's him."

A flicker of relief crossed Durga's face. "Thank you, sir. I promise to do my best and be on good terms with him."

Mohan gave her a pointed look. "Rudra has gone through hell since losing Nandini. He left everything behind to take care of her family. That's not the kind of loss from which one easily recovers. Be mindful of that if you are going to work with him.

"I understand, sir," Durga said seriously. "Thank you for trusting me with this opportunity,"

Mohan nodded, his face relaxing just enough to indicate an end to the conversation. "Now, let's make some headway with this case, Durga. We can't afford to waste a single minute," he told her.

With one more nod, Durga took her leave of the cabin, her steps measured but purposeful, determination burning brighter than ever in her eyes.

The police station buzzed with the low hum of activity—phones ringing, papers shuffling, and muted conversations filling the air. Sashi sat in a stiff wooden chair; his hands clasped tightly in his lap. His face bore the unmistakable lines of stress and exhaustion, his eyes scanning the room nervously. Every creak of the door made him flinch, his thoughts undoubtedly on edge.

An officer approached, his uniform crisp and demeanour composed. "Please come," Officer Khaleel said, gesturing towards the hallway leading to the interrogation rooms.

Sashi stood, his movements sluggish as though the weight of his circumstances dragged him down. He followed Khaleel, his footsteps echoing down the tiled corridor, each one a step closer to the unknown.

Inside the interrogation room, Rudra sat waiting. His posture was calm but commanding. His elbows rested on the table, and his fingers tapped rhythmically as if in thought. His sharp eyes were fixed on the door as it opened, and Sashi stepped inside.

"Please, come in," Rudra said, his voice steady yet not unkind.

Sashi hesitated briefly before sitting across from him, his shoulders hunched as if bracing for what was to come. The room was stark, with harsh lighting and an air of formality that heightened the tension. Khaleel entered behind him, taking up a spot near the wall, his arms crossed as he observed silently.

Sashi's voice was barely above a whisper when he spoke. "Is there any news?"

Rudra shook his head, his expression grave. "Nothing yet."

The response made Sashi's face fall further, his hands gripping the edge of the table tightly. Rudra leaned forward slightly, his gaze intent but not intimidating.

"How are you coping?" Rudra asked, his tone softer now.

Sashi exhaled a shaky breath. "I don't know... I'm left alone with my daughter. She keeps asking about her mother, and I have no answers."

"I know this is an incredibly difficult time for you and your daughter," Rudra said, his voice calm but firm. "But your help is crucial. We need to get to the bottom of this, and every detail you can provide might make the difference."

Sashi nodded slowly; his movements mechanical. "I just want to know who did this... and why. Why her?"

Rudra leaned in further, his hands clasped together on the table. His tone became resolute, almost urgent. "We need to ask you some questions about your wife—about her life, her relationships, anything that might help us understand who could have done this."

"I'll tell you everything I know," Sashi said immediately, his desperation clear.

Rudra nodded, acknowledging the man's willingness. "Did she mention anything unusual recently? Anything about someone new in her life?"

Sashi's brows furrowed as he processed the question. "What do you mean by 'anyone new in her life'?" he asked, his voice tinged with confusion and a hint of defensiveness.

Rudra's eyes remained steady, unwavering. "Sashi, the bodies we've recovered so far... they're of a male and a female together. We're trying to establish connections, relationships, anything that might link them."

Sashi sat back slightly, his breath hitching. "She used to work for a shipping company," he began after a moment's pause, his voice flat and devoid of emotion. "But after we had our daughter, she left the job to take care of her." He paused again, his fingers gripping the table harder. "Since then, she's been a homemaker. She was always with our daughter."

Rudra studied him carefully, weighing his words. "Are you sure there was no one from her past, perhaps someone she reconnected with recently?"

"No," Sashi said, shaking his head firmly. "She was devoted to our family. She barely went out unless it was for errands or to take our daughter to school."

Rudra glanced briefly at Khaleel, who remained stoic, then returned his gaze to Sashi. "And what about her phone or social media? Did you notice any unusual activity there?"

Sashi seemed to think for a moment before shaking his head again. "I didn't check her phone often. She wasn't very active online. She would post pictures of our daughter sometimes, but that's all."

The room fell silent for a beat, the tension palpable. Rudra's fingers resumed their quiet tapping on the table as he considered the next line of questioning. The man in front of him seemed genuine, his grief raw, but Rudra knew from experience that the smallest details could be the key to cracking a case.

"I understand this is painful," Rudra said after a pause, his tone gentler now. "But we're doing everything we can to find answers. For you, for your daughter, and for your wife."

Sashi's eyes glistened with unshed tears, but he held them back, his lips pressed into a thin line. "Please," he said, his voice breaking slightly. "Find whoever did this. Make them pay."

"We will," Rudra said firmly, his words carrying the weight of a promise. "But I need you to stay strong and cooperate with us. If anything, else comes to mind, no matter how small, let us know immediately."

Sashi nodded, his resolve returning as he straightened in his chair. "I will," he said, his voice firmer now. "I'll do whatever it takes to help."

The room itself felt heavier, as though the air was thickening, with an even more frenetic current of tension inside it now. Rudra's voice broke the silence, low and deliberate.

"As you told me earlier, your wife quit her job when your daughter was born. But, Sashi," Rudra's tone turned hard, his eyes unyielding, "who was she texting and meeting all this while?"

Sashi furrowed his brow, his puzzlement real as he looked up at Rudra. "What are you talking about?" he asked, his voice laced with bewilderment and a dash of defensiveness.

Without a word, Rudra pushed a set of papers across the table. The crisp sheets halted in front of Sashi, who gazed at them for a moment before hesitantly picking them up. His eyes scanned the columns of phone records, numbers listed on the page with which he was completely unfamiliar and unsettling. His confusion deepened as his eyes flicked back to Rudra, who watched him with an expression that was both probing and sceptical.

Do you recall any of these numbers?" Rudra asked, his voice firm but not aggressive. "Please, look carefully.

Sashi's hands quivered slightly as he flipped through the pages. His lips moved silently as he vainly tried to recall any of the sequences of digits. Finally, with a slow, deliberate head shake as if realisation hit him in waves, he said: "Sir, I don't know what these numbers are. Trust me, I really don't know who they are."

Rudra's eyes narrowed, his lips pressing into a thin line. He leaned back in his chair, his fingers tapping rhythmically on the edge of the table. "There's one number in particular," he said, his voice dropping an octave, "that she used to call every day. Every single day, Sashi. And yet, you're telling me you had no idea about this?"

The accusation just hung in the air, a storm cloud that weighed down upon Sashi. His face crumpled as he looked at Rudra, desperation etched into every line of his features. "Sir," he said, his voice cracking, "I'm telling you the truth. I don't know anything about this. Why would I lie? We have a daughter. Why would I do anything that would make her lose her mother?" His voice rose slightly, the emotion threatening to spill over. "I loved my wife. She was everything to me."

Rudra didn't blink. His face was an unreadable mask, his eyes riveted to Sashi's face, intent on unearthing some truth hidden there. After a while, he sighed and exhaled slowly. It was more a sound of resignation than of relief. "Sorry," he said, his voice soft but with an edge. "But I don't think your wife felt anything for you like that."

The words hit Sashi like a physical blow. His body slumped forward into the chair, his face crumpling as he began to cry. He tried to wipe away the tears with the back of his hand as hastily as possible as if to force himself not to cry. His shoulders heaved as he tried to regain his composure, and his laboured breathing filled the silence in the room.

Rudra picked up the glass of water sitting on the table and pushed it towards Sashi. The action was purposeful, almost mechanical. "Here," he said simply.

Sashi tentatively reached out, his hand shaking as he lifted the glass. He sipped just a little water from it, with which the tumult within him was not content, and then set it back on the table with a soft clink. No words were spoken by either of them for a moment. Rudra observed him with an unreadable expression, while Sashi stared down at his hands, the focus of his gaze unfocused.

And finally, it was Rudra who broke the silence. His tone was composed but unmistakably laced with authority. "I'm going to let you go for now," he said, leaning forward slightly to emphasise his point. "But listen to me carefully, Sashi. Do not leave the city. Stay put until we tell you otherwise." With a stiff motion, Sashi lifted his body up. He stood and paced gently across the room towards the door.

Breaking his motion, Rudra said, "Can I have your phone?" His tone made concessions impossible.

Sashi blinked, totally caught off guard. "Sorry...?" he replied, his voice full of confusion.

Rudra repeated himself, this time with a touch more insistence. "Can you please hand over the phone?"

He hesitated for a moment before slowly pulling his phone out of his pocket and placing it on the table. Officer Khaleel, standing silently nearby, advanced forward to claim the item. He was commanding and graceful in his movement as he reached out for the device.

"Password," Khaleel curtly demanded. Then, without waiting, he repeated more forcefully, "PASSWORD."

Sashi hesitated for a heartbeat, then dully replied, "1014. It's her birthday."

The room seemed to freeze for a moment, and it was almost as if the sudden addition of a password to the dialogue gave an unsaid depth to the conversation. Khaleel nodded curtly and inputted the code into the phone before locking it.

"We'll hand it back once we're done with the investigation," Khaleel said, his tone devoid of emotion, his focus already back on the case.

Sashi stood, the leaden drag in his movements telling so much about the storm inside. He didn't say a word; instead, he turned to the door and began walking towards it, his movements languid and staccato. He stopped right beside it for the briefest flash of a moment, as if collecting himself before turning the door handle to let himself out. It clicked shut, the noise of which echoed in the otherwise still room.

Khaleel looked at Rudra, furrowing his brow as if thinking. "Sir," he started hesitantly, "do you think he has anything to do with the murder? He had to, didn't he?"

Rudra leaned back in his chair and tapped the fingers of the hand resting on the table's edge. His face said nothing as he thought about the question. And finally, he spoke, his voice measured and thoughtful. "I don't think so. But you never know," he added, his gaze distantly focused on something afar. "Anything is possible."

The weight of Rudra's words hovered in the air, sobering one to the uncertainty that went with the investigation. Khaleel nodded slowly; his face a mixture of doubt and determination had passed across it.

The nightlife throbbed around the city streets; a couple strolled down the sidewalk beside them, her voice and his chuckled laughter merging into the general city sound. They seemed completely oblivious to the world around them, their concentration so utterly channelled into each other.

But watching them from the shadows was someone.

A dark van crept down the street, its movements slow and deliberate. The vehicle stopped suddenly near the couple, its engine purring low and menacing. The couple paused for a moment, their faces changing as an unspoken unease settled over them. The streetlights cast long shadows, making tension seem to double as the van's door began to slide open.

Chapter 4

Intertwined Lives

The police station was abuzz with activity the following day. Desks were cluttered with heaps of paperwork, phones rang incessantly, and officers moved with purpose. Durga, a determined young reporter, approached the station, clutching a folded note in her hand. Her steps were brisk as she approached Rudra and Khaleel, who sat at the desk absorbed in conversation.

Sir," Durga said, her voice steady but urgent. "I found this note on your jeep."

She presented the note to Rudra. He took it without hesitation, furrowing his brow as he opened the paper. He quickly scanned the contents before shifting from confusion to alarm. The air seemed to thicken with tension as he rose abruptly from his chair.

Not a word was needed. Rudra ran towards the jeep, urgent and swift on his feet. Khaleel and Durga exchanged another glance, their curiosity peaked but loyalty never wavering. They ran behind him, ready for whatever awaited them outside. The weight of the note still sits in their minds, a new piece in this ever-growing puzzle that becomes more complicated with each passing second.

Rudra ran out of the station doors, his strides hasty as he made his way toward his jeep. His sharp eyes flitted about, scanning the street and nearby alleys for a glimpse of the person who left the note. Durga, Khaleel, and Ali trailed closely behind him. Curiosity and resolve sat upon their faces in equal measure.

Durga caught up with him, her breath held as she asked, "Sir, did you see anybody?"

Not breaking his stride, Rudra snapped back, "Durga, did you notice anyone?"

She shook her head quickly. "No, sir."

Rudra growled under his breath before raising his voice a little more to say, "Let's move."

In one fluid motion, he climbed into the jeep's driver's seat, his hands grasping tightly onto the steering wheel as if willing to assist him in finding the answers. Khaleel and Ali also settled into the vehicle without an argument. The sound of the engine roaring awakened Durga's faint voice.

"Sir, can I come along with you? Please!" she pleaded, running toward the jeep.

And Khaleel, frustrated with the entire situation, turned towards her. "Durga, it's not possible. This is no ordinary errand."

But Durga wouldn't let up. She took a step closer, her voice rising in desperation. "Please, sir. Please let me come."

Rudra shrugged, his patience all but stretched to its limits, but then looked into her set face and relented. "Fine. But don't touch any of the evidence at the crime scene," he warned sternly.

She nodded eagerly and climbed in, sitting down with silent determination. The jeep tore into the crowded streets. Rudra's mind was racing ahead of the jeep, trying to make sense of the ominous note addressed to him.

The jeep screeched to a stop outside an abandoned factory whose rusted shell left little to the imagination. Three officers emerged, their purposeful strides assessing the whole scene. Before them stood the silent spectre of the building - desolate in its cracked windows and peeling paint.

Rudra led the group inside, his footsteps echoing ominously against the cold, empty walls. The factory smelled of dampness and iron, the latter growing stronger as they ventured deeper.

As they moved, the trail of blood on the floor became apparent and pulled them into the heart of the building. The footsteps of the group paused momentarily, their boots hitting the concrete quieted by the weight of the discovery ahead. Blood smeared and splattered across the ground painted a grim picture of what had gone on.

In the middle of the room were two chairs, where the man's and the woman's slumped bodies lay lifeless. The couple's faces were so battered as to be unrecognisable, their hands tied tightly behind them. To the side of the scene, almost casually placed, there was a small box with the word "*KAALI*" scribbled boldly on it. Atop this little box was a phone - the screen was dark, but it was ominously present.

Rudra donned a pair of gloves - the snap of the material breaking the silent tension. He approached the box and gently plucked the phone from inside. The screen flickered to life as he unlocked it, revealing a video file. He looked at the others, his face unreadable, and then pressed play.

The group stood behind him, their breath stuck in their throats, as the video began playing.

———

Grainy and yet vivid, the footage portrayed the horror. It displayed the same couple, tied to their chairs as they were now. Their faces were battered, blood streaming down from wounds visible even through the poor quality of the recording. The man and woman squirmed desperately, their muffled screams piercing the stillness of the factory.

The camera zoomed in on their tear-streaked faces, capturing every detail of their anguish.

———

Hours later, in the meeting room of the Commissioner's office, the grim video played again, this time on a big screen dominating one entire wall. Rudra sat at the head of the long, heavy table; jaw tensed as he stared at the screen. Commissioner Krishna Reddy sat nearby, his hands clasped in front of him, his face grave. Khaleel sat beside Rudra, and Ali stood behind them with arms crossed, his eyes glued to the horrific footage.

The glow of the screen illuminated the room, casting long shadows on the walls. Everyone in the room watched with rapt attention, their faces betraying varying degrees of horror, anger, and determination.

When the video ended, Krishna Reddy leaned back in his chair, his expression hardened. "Rudra," he said, his voice steady but laced with frustration, "I think the killer is mocking us by giving us this video."

Rudra nodded slowly, his gaze never leaving the darkened screen. "I think so too, sir. The killer isn't just mocking us; he's challenging us. He wants us to know he's in control."

Krishna Reddy turned to Rudra; his brow furrowed. "Have you identified the victims?"

"Yes, Sir," replied Rudra. "They are a married couple. They even have a five-year-old daughter."

The weight of those words hung heavily in the room, and the personal devastation they left in the wake of the killer was starkly illustrated by them. Rudra took a deep breath and continued, with his tone resolute. "Sir, the killer seems to be targeting women with children."

He pressed a button on the console in front of him, and pictures of the victims began to slide down the screen. Their smiling faces at happier moments made for a particularly cruel juxtaposition with what all eyes had seen on that video.

Krishna Reddy studied the photos intently, his expression unreadable. The silence in the room was thick, each officer lost in their thoughts, each grappling with the enormity of the case before them.

Rudra stood at the front of the dimly lit meeting room, his posture rigid, every word he spoke carrying the weight of responsibility. The glow of the large screen illuminated his face, deepening the lines of exhaustion and focus etched onto it. On the screen, the photo of the first victim—a woman with a faint, forced smile—was displayed.

"The first victim," Rudra began, his voice steady but edged with a grim undertone, "is a prostitute. She has a son."

The room was silent, the only sound being the faint hum of the projector as it shifted to display the next photo. A second woman's face appeared on the screen. Her features were softer, her eyes carrying the warmth of a homemaker.

Rudra gestured to the image. "The second victim is a homemaker. She has a daughter."

He paused for a moment, letting the information sink in before clicking to the next slide. The third photo replaced the second – a couple, their smiles frozen in a moment of happiness that now felt haunting.

"And these two," Rudra continued, his voice lowering slightly, "are married to each other. They also have a daughter."

Rudra took a step back, his eyes scanning the room briefly before gesturing to Ali to switch on the lights. The sudden brightness filled the space, breaking the sombre trance, the dim lighting and gruesome details had created. Rudra's gaze shifted back to Commissioner Krishna Reddy, who had been watching intently, his arms crossed and his expression grave.

"Why," Rudra asked aloud, the question cutting through the silence, "is the killer targeting people who have kids? What is the pattern? The motive?"

Krishna Reddy straightened slightly in his chair; his brow furrowed as if contemplating the same question. Finally, he spoke. "What's your next plan of action, Rudra?"

Rudra folded his arms, his mind already working through the steps ahead. "Sir, for now, we are interrogating the family members of the victims to see if any of them could be involved in the murders. But I doubt it. The murder pattern is consistent across all the cases, and it feels personal—like the killer has some connection or vendetta."

Krishna Reddy pushed his chair back and rose, his presence commanding as he spoke. "Call the family members in for questioning again. See if they can recall anything—any small detail that might help us connect the dots."

"Yes, Sir," Rudra replied firmly, his tone conveying his readiness to follow through.

The bright daylight washed over the driveway of Rudra's house as he, Anvi, her grandmother, and Officer Khaleel stood together, preparing to leave. The warmth of the sun contrasted sharply with the cold sense of unease that lingered from the investigation. Rudra glanced at the others, ensuring everyone was ready.

The sound of a bike approaching broke the stillness, drawing their attention. Durga pulled up, the engine of her bike rumbling before she killed it and stepped off. She removed her helmet, shaking loose her hair as her eyes locked onto Rudra's.

"Sorry, sir, I'm late," she said, a mix of guilt and apology in her voice. "I got stuck at the office."

Khaleel, standing nearby with his arms loosely crossed, frowned slightly. "Durga, you should have at least called us. We were waiting for you."

Rudra's tone was calmer, his usual intensity softened by the familial atmosphere around them. "It's okay," he said, brushing off Khaleel's frustration with a wave of his hand. "But we're heading out now. We can catch up later."

Durga's gaze shifted briefly to Anvi and the grandmother before she nodded. "I didn't know you all were going out," she replied, her voice subdued. "I'll come back later."

The grandmother, who had been observing the exchange quietly, stepped forward, her tone warm and inviting. "We're taking Anvi out," she said. "Why don't you join us, Durga?"

Durga hesitated, her hand still holding her helmet. "No, Auntie," she said politely, shaking her head. "You all carry on. Maybe another time."

The grandmother wasn't one to give up easily. She turned to Rudra, her tone firm but affectionate. "Rudra, why don't you tell her? She'll listen to you."

Rudra glanced at Durga, who was clearly torn between her hesitation and the invitation. He gave her a faint smile and said, "Durga, please join us. It'll be nice to have you along."

Before Durga could respond, Rudra turned to Khaleel. "Khaleel, why don't you join us too?"

Khaleel shook his head, his smile apologetic yet resolute. "No, Sir. You all carry on. I need to help my uncle with something."

Without waiting for further persuasion, Khaleel mounted his bike and started the engine. He gave them a brief wave before driving off, leaving the group standing in the driveway.

Durga watched him go, her fingers tightening slightly on her helmet before she finally nodded. "Alright, Sir," she said quietly. "I'll join you."

Rudra's lips curled into a faint, approving smile as he gestured towards the vehicle. The grandmother, satisfied, patted Durga's shoulder lightly. Anvi clung to her grandmother's hand, her small face lighting up at the prospect of having Durga along. Together, they began making their way towards the car, the subtle tension of the earlier moments fading into the anticipation of a simple outing.

She came towards the car with a smile that seemed to transmit pure joy. She lit up the driveway, where Rudra, Anvi, and their grandmother stood getting ready to leave. The grandmother looked up and greeted her warmly; Rudra, standing beside the car, gave her a nod, along with a smile.

Durga stepped into the car without any hesitation. She still smiled as brightly as ever. Glancing at Rudra, her eyes sparkled with excitement. She radiated energy that pushed him to return her smile, though he was muted. He flicked his eyes to the rearview mirror for the briefest of moments, ensuring everyone was settled before he started the engine.

The streets of the city were filled with the vibrancy of people living, as Rudra waded his way through the traffic. The noise from the street vendors and the cars in the distance forming a loud noise gave way to a background to work within. Durga sat in the back seat with Anvi; she was already bouncing with excitement.

Durga leaned forward, her voice small but energetic and full of electricity. "Anvi, wanna play a game?"

Anvi's eyes lit up, and she nodded eagerly. "Yes, Durga *Didi*! What game?"

Durga pretended to think for a moment, tapping her chin theatrically. "Alright, how about a guessing game? I'll describe something, and you guess what it is."

Anvi clapped her hands, giggling. "Okay! I'm ready."

As the game commenced, laughter bubbled from the back seat, filling the car with a cheerful ambiance. Durga's descriptions were vivid and often silly, and Anvi's guesses grew wilder with each turn, much to their mutual delight. Rudra, although focused on driving, couldn't help but glance in the rearview mirror. He caught Durga's eyes briefly as she looked up at him, her smile softening for a moment before she returned her attention to Anvi.

The connection was short-lived yet unmistakable, silent comprehension passing between them. Durga's elation at that moment was real, and Rudra found himself smiling involuntarily before shifting his gaze back to the road.

As they reached the shopping mall, Rudra smoothly turned the car into the parking lot. He looked up carefully to find a suitable spot convenient for the grandmother. The car halted, and one by one they began to climb out.

Anvi jumped to Durga's side at once and placed her hand in hers. Her face was beaming from ear to ear, excitement radiating from her every step. "Durga *Didi*, are we going first to the toy shop?" she asked eagerly.

The laughter spilled from Durga's lips as she squeezed Anvi's hand gently. "Let's see what Rudra Sir says."

Rudra stepped out of the driver's window with a loose posture but a hard look that met Durga briefly before he turned to the grandmother to make sure she was fine as she adjusted her dupatta. Together, they entered the bustling mall.

Inside, the air was filled with the buzz of families and children, their laughter echoing against the polished floors. Bright lights and vibrant displays created an inviting atmosphere, and Anvi's excitement seemed to double. She tugged at Durga's hand, her tiny feet almost skipping as she pointed to a nearby toy shop adorned with colourful displays.

"Durga *Didi*, look! Look at all the toys!" Anvi exclaimed, her voice carrying an uncontainable thrill.

Durga crouched a little to match the child's height, grinning warmly. "Shall we take a closer look?"

Anvi nodded enthusiastically and asked Rudra to go ahead, entering the toy shop that was filled with an assortment of toys in every colour under the sun. Anvi ran from aisle to aisle, her laughter out blaring as she found a miniature dollhouse, puzzles, and games. Durga followed closely behind, her smile never faltering as she indulged the child's excitement.

When they came out, Rudra walked with a brightly coloured bag of treasures Anvi had picked, slung over his shoulder. Anvi skipped beside him, grasping Durga's hand tightly. The grandmother strolled leisurely beside them, her eyes soft with watchfulness.

Around the corner, colourful arcade games of the children's play area came into view. Anvi opened her eyes wide with delight; she broke free from Durga's hand to run to a colourful game. "Durga *Didi*, come on!" she called, urging her newfound friend to join her.

Durga laughed, her steps quickening to keep up with Anvi's boundless energy. She crouched beside the little girl at the arcade game, guiding her through the controls as the screen lit up with cheerful animations. Rudra leaned against a nearby railing, arms crossed, watching the scene unfold with a rare softness in his expression.

Time flew by as the group only filled their schedules with good-natured kidding around and laughter. When it was actually time to leave, they headed back into the parking lot. The earlier vibrancy of the mall had somewhat toned down with the gently soothing feeling of the evening.

Smiling still, they walked towards the car. Anvi gripped Durga's hand tightly. She smiled serenely, seemingly content. Rudra unlocked the doors. Anvi's grandmother sat in the front seat before turning to Durga and Anvi. He opened the back door for them, and both climbed in, settling in comfortably as the car roared back to life.

It was totally peaceful on the way back to Rudra's house with the city lights casting a warm glow against the windows. Durga leaned back in her seat, occasionally looking sideways at Rudra, still and focused on the road before them. Anvi was tired from the adventures of the day and rested her head against Durga's arm, her eyelids growing heavier with each passing moment.

By the time they arrived, he parked the car in the driveway with his usual care. The first to step out was the grandmother who stretched slightly as she opened the door to the house. Rudra followed, his steps deliberate, helping half-asleep Anvi out of the car. Durga lingered for a moment, watching the scene with a faint smile.

As they entered the house, the familiar warmth welcomed them back into its embrace, and the evening's soft hush retained the memories of the day.

The warm candlelight of the house beckoned to her and made Durga feel contented when she entered the house. She beamed with joy at Anvi and the grandmother; her voice was melodious and full of true warmth.

"I had such a wonderful time today. Thank you," she said, her gratitude evident in every word.

Durga bent forward and hugged Anvi closely in a warm embrace. She then approached the grandmother and hugged her in the same way. The grandmother smiled fondly at the young woman who had been watching her all day.

"Why don't you stay for some time and then go?" the grandma kept suggesting, with a tender but firm tone.

Before Durga could respond, Anvi tugged at her hand, her eyes pleading. "Please stay, *didi*. Just for a little while?" she asked, her voice full of innocent hope.

Durga looked at the two of them, her hesitation melting away in the face of their sincerity. "Okay," she agreed softly, unable to resist Anvi's earnest request.

Anvi's face brightened, and she tugged Durga's hand to lead her to her room. "Come! I'll show you my favourite toy!" was her excited shriek in a voice as tiny as it was shrill.

It was just after a while when, in the kitchen, the aroma of freshly brewed coffee filled the air with its soothing goodness. Durga watched as the grandmother poured the steaming liquid into delicate cups. It was so quiet in that kitchen that only an occasional clinking of the cups against the counter would shatter the stillness there.

The elderly woman glanced at Durga with a warm smile. "Anvi slept, did she?" she asked in a soft, motherly voice.

Durga nodded. "Yes, Aunty. As soon as I tucked her in, she slept almost immediately," she replied, her voice warm and brimming with affection for the small child.

The grandmother looked at Durga for a while, with eyes filled with gratitude. "After such a long time, I am seeing Rudra this happy," she said in a very quiet tone. "Thanks, Durga."

Durga gave her a small smile, as a mix of different emotions set swirling inside her. She watched as the grandmother took a cup and walked away, taking Durga along to be alone with her own thoughts.

Later that night, the terrace was washed in soft moonlight. Stars were scattered like tiny jewels across the sky as a cool breeze rustled through the trees below, carrying gentle murmurs of the night. Rudra stood near the edge of the terrace, framed against the distant lights of the city. He stood easily, his face showing a great deal that he was not saying aloud: his line of eyes on the horizon, as if seeking answers to the confusion within.

Durga stepped onto the terrace, her presence quiet but unmistakable. She carried two steaming cups of coffee, the warmth of the mugs contrasting with the cool night air. Her footsteps were light, but Rudra turned at the sound, his features softening slightly when he saw her.

"I thought you might need this," Durga said, offering him one of the cups with a gentle smile.

He took the cup from her, his fingers rasping against hers briefly. "Thanks," he said simply, an undertone of weariness in his voice.

Durga tilted her head slightly, studying him with quiet curiosity. "What's Anvi doing?" he asked suddenly, breaking the silence between them.

"She's been put to bed," Durga said softly, her voice calm but warm. Her lips broke into a fleeting smile as she drank some of her coffee, and her gaze wandered up to the skyline.

They stood there for a moment, side by side, the stillness stretching between them yet somehow comfortingly silent. The faint rustle of leaves and the distant thrum of the city provided a soothing background.

Then Durga broke the stillness, her voice soft but deliberate. "I like you," she said, the words spilling from her lips before she could reconsider her words.

He turned to her sharply, his brows furrowing. "What?" he asked, disbelief in his voice.

Durga looked at him steadily, her expression unflinching despite the vulnerability in her voice. "I didn't know how to tell you in a better way, but I like you."

Rudra let out a disbelieving laugh, shaking his head. "Do you hear yourself? How can you even think like that?" he asked, his tone incredulous.

"I don't know," Durga said, her voice cracking. "I just know that I like you. I know what you must be thinking—that if I come into your life, what will happen to Anvi? But I promise you, I will take care of Anvi like a mother."

Rudra glared at her, his facial expression one of anger and confusion. "You know everything, and still?" he asked, his voice rising.

I know," Durga said firmly, now. "I know even you like me, but you're hiding it. I swear to God, Rudra, I will take care of Anvi. Trust me."

Rudra's jaw locked into place, and he flicked his gaze away, not at her now, but at the cup he held in his hand. "Can you just leave me alone?" he said finally in a voice that was cold and dismissive.

Durga's heart contracted at his words, but she did not speak. Without a word, she wheeled and disappeared from the terrace, her steps hastening, unsteady. Her eyes went dim with black tears; she almost collided with the grandmother, standing there in the doorway, her face unsearchable.

Durga stopped, shocked, and they said nothing for a moment. And then Durga moved forward and hugged the grandmother closely, sobbing silently in the embrace. The old woman held her there for a moment, her hands gentle but strong, before Durga pulled back and ran down the stairs, leaving the older woman standing there, lost in quiet thought.

Back on the balcony, Rudra froze. He sipped his coffee, which had turned lukewarm by now, and slowly followed through. His eyes returned to the city lights twinkling below, but his mind wasn't focused. The cool breeze rustled his hair as he stood alone beneath the vast expanse of the starlit sky, the weight of unspoken words and unacknowledged emotions pressing heavily on him.

—◦—

The dim glow of the computer screen cast long shadows across Rudra's room. The room was quiet, except for the silent hum of the monitor and the occasional shuffle of papers on the desk. Rudra sat motionless, his eyes glued to the images displayed before him. Crime scene photographs filled the screen; each was a piece in a grim narrative. His brow furrowed in concentration, he was racing his mind to find a minute detail that was overlooked. Every photo in the trays spoke a haunting tale, and Rudra bore the weight of unearthing those truths.

Suddenly, there was a knock on the door that snapped him out of stillness, shrill and startling. Rudra blinked, a bit drawn away from his thoughts, and focused on the door.

"Come in," he said, his voice steady but tinged with curiosity.

The door creaked open slowly, revealing the familiar figure of Anvi's grandmother. She entered the room with a gentle smile, her eyes soft and filled with an understanding that only years of wisdom could bring. Her presence, as always, was a comforting balm in the midst of his turmoil.

Rudra stood up right away, leaving the desk with all those grim images on the screen. He crossed the room and met her; there, together, they crossed over to the bed where they sat side by side. Silently or heavily but not uncomfortably, as each had known the importance of what was about to be said.

"Are you okay?" asked his grandmother in a voice low and tender.

Rudra nodded, though his expression betrayed a deeper weariness. "I'm okay, Mom," he replied, using the term of endearment he'd always called her. "Just going through some tough cases."

She placed a comforting hand on his shoulder, her touch steady and reassuring. "I wanted to tell you something," she began hesitantly, her tone carrying the weight of her emotions. "But I'm not sure how you will react."

Rudra turned towards her, his eyes locking with hers in an unyielding gaze. "Mom, just tell me. You know

I'll never say no to you," he said, his voice firm, but a tender feeling was present in it.

Her hand stayed on his shoulder as she deeply inhaled. "It's... it's about Durga," she said, softly admitting this as her voice dropped slightly. "She's a very nice girl, Rudra. And I overheard your conversation with her earlier. She really likes you, and I don't think you should let her go."

Rudra's jaw locked up, and he turned his face aside, staring at the ground as if he could find an answer somewhere in its textures. "Mom, you know it can't happen," he said softly but persuasively.

"Why?" she asked softly, tilting her head to watch him. "Because of us?"

"Yes," Rudra said firmly. "You both are my responsibility, and I just can't bring someone else into my life."

Anvi's grandmother's eyes softened even more, her face a combination of love and concern. "You know I won't be here forever to take care of you and Anvi," she said softly. "I just want you and Anvi to have someone. Someone who will love and care for you the way you both deserve."

Rudra looked at her, his lips pressing into a thin line. The weight of her words settled heavily on his shoulders, but he remained silent.

"She knows about you," Anvi's grandmother continued, her voice unwavering. "And I'm certain she will take care of you both."

Rudra opened his mouth to speak, but no words came out. It was a battle for his heart, duty pitted against the faintest flicker of longing. After a moment, he only bowed his head, the tension in his posture betraying the storm raging within him.

Anvi's grandmother squeezed his shoulder softly. It was without words, yet full of encouragement and love. She got up from the bed and stepped slowly to the door. Her footsteps were light but deliberate in their own quiet way. As she reached the doorway, she paused, then turned back to glance at him. Her gaze lingered a moment, pent up with unspoken feelings. Then, in silence, she stepped out and closed the door softly with a click.

Rudra alone in the room was once again wrapped in silence. He turned his head back to the monitor, where all the captured crime scene images remained stiff like photographs. Yet, the images on those captured frames were no longer in his head; instead, it was Anvi's grandmother's words that "whispered" in his head. He leaned back in the chair, looking up at the ceiling as he wrestled with the responsibility versus the faint possibility of something more.

The room seemed small now, the air heavy. The images on the monitor, which once screamed for his attention, were now distantly and desperately unimportant. Rudra sat there with his mind churning in a haze of dim light, alone bearing the weight of decisions he was uncertain whether he was ready for.

...✍

Chapter 5

The Unravelling Truth

Very quietly, turning the doorknob, the quiet click of the latch punctuated the quietude of the room. Rudra stepped inside softly, opening the door; his nonobtrusive entrance was as if he did not wish to intrude on a fragile moment. A nightlight cast an enveloping warmth in soft amber; Anvi was rolled into her blanket, her little body all tucked away. Sleep swelled in and out with each respective breath, and a serene face beamed from her calm slumber.

He stepped closer, every step cautious, and sat down at the foot of the bed. The mattress plunged under his weight, but still, Anvi did not wake up. For a moment, he just looked at her, his facial muscles relaxing in the low light. Reaching out with a gentle touch, he caressed her small hand with his own. Her fingers were warm, delicate, and comforting, reminding him of innocence and love in such a harsh world.

As Rudra gripped her hand, Anvi shifted slightly. Her eyelids fluttered open, and her lashes rose to reveal sleepy eyes, slivers of bright sparkle shining there even in the darkness. A slow, drowsy smile spread over her face, her lips curving in recognition of the figure beside her. She neither spoke nor opened her eyes but reached out for him, wrapping her arms around him in a half-asleep, affectionate embrace. Rudra leaned into her hug, feeling the weight of the world lift, if only for a moment.

Her voice was barely a whisper, her words melting into the stillness. "You're here," she murmured.

"I'm here," he said softly, his tone steady yet filled with emotion. He rested his chin lightly on her head as her breathing evened out once more. She drifted back into slumber, her arms slackening around him.

The room was ageless; a pocket of peace Rudra wished he could stay in for eternity. But moments like these were fleeting; reality always had its way of pulling him back.

A knock on the door broke into that stillness. Rudra's eyes opened, straining as he half-awakened. Blinking a couple of times to clear his head, he looked down to find Anvi below him. Gently, he slid his hand from around hers and set it on the bed beside her. Her chest rose and fell steadily, its motion completely unreactive to the commotion.

The knock came once again, this time insistent on being answered. Rudra sat forward, his movements at pains to be silent and not make more noise than necessary. He stood up and walked toward the door, flung it open, and right in front of it stood Anvi's grandmother. Her face was serenely calm but conveyed a gravity that Rudra sensed immediately.

Wordlessly, she thrust the phone at him. Rudra took it, holding it to his ear. "Hello?" he said, his voice flat but wary.

The voice on the other end was raspy, full of tension and urgency. Instantly, Rudra's face changed, growing harder, as if that news was a punch in the gut. He didn't say anything, allowing the voice on the other end to continue with his tightened grip on the phone.

By the time he gave the receiver back to Anvi's grandmother, his face was impassive, but there was a storm brewing in his eyes. A brief nod was given to her before he stepped past her and walked out briskly from the room.

The scene sort of dissolved into chaos in his mind as he pieced together the fragments of what he had just heard. Somewhere across town, under the shadow of an under-construction building, police officers had gathered. Durga stood amidst the turmoil, clutching a knife, her face pale but determined. The night air had grown heavy with tension, and the scene was bathed in the harsh glare of police lights.

Rudra burst into the police station; there was an intensity in his eyes combined with a sense of urgency and worry. His footsteps echoed down the sterile hallway as he went to face them. The officers around him turned their heads as he moved with purpose, and he went to the desk where an officer was sorting through paperwork. "Where is Durga?" His voice was sharp and demanding, holding no room for hesitation.

The officer looked up, momentarily startled. "We've placed her in the interrogation room," he replied.

Without another word, he gestured to the police officer to move ahead. Along with him, they stepped down the corridor, the heavy air growing with each step. When they arrived at the interrogation room, Rudra stood at the small window in the door peering in. Inside, he saw Durga seated on a cold metal chair. Her shoulders tensed forward, and her face was a mix of defiance and fear. On the opposite side of Durga sat Khaleel. Measured but probing were the words to describe his demeanour.

"Who gave you the information about Durga?" Rudra asked, his voice quieter now but still insistent.

The officer gestured towards the waiting area. "The witness is sitting outside, sir."

Rudra nodded and followed the officer to the bench where a middle-aged man sat. The man, in his fifties, looked weathered and uneasy, his fingers fidgeting as he recognised Rudra approaching. When Rudra and the officer halted in front of him, the man rose hastily, his nervousness betraying his jerky movements.

"Tell me what you saw," Rudra commanded in a voice that was steady but firm.

The man gulped hard, looking around between Rudra and the officer. His eyes darted all around as if looking for the right phrase to utter. He finally started talking.

"I was going to sleep," the man said, his voice quivering a little. "Right outside an old building, you know. It is where I always spend the night." He talked with his hands as if to recall the scene. "I had settled down when I saw that one girl," he went on. "She was running really fast and someone… somebody chased her."

He gasped, breath catching. He seemed to relive the moment. Rudra waited, his gaze unyielding, urging the man to continue.

"That person," the man spoke on, voice lowered now, "he was holding a knife. It was dark, but I could see the blade. I—I didn't know what to do. So, I called the police."

The words dangled in the air, holding the weight of syllables in implication. Rudra stood there unmoving, his mind racing as he connected the dots. The man's account painted pictures, but the edges were still just blurry, the truth unrevealed.

As the man sat back down, slouching his shoulders, Rudra stood up straight. He thought of Durga and clenched his jaw, his expression hardening into determination. Whatever was true, he had to find it.

The police station's fluorescent lights cast a pale, stark glow upon the scene, heavy with tension. He stood tall, his sharp eyes fixed on a man. A witness of middle age, wiry frame, and worried look fidgeted under Rudra's piercing gaze.

"Are you certain that it was her?" Rudra asked, but with a voice-controlled, though an edge of scepticism crept onto his tongue.

The witness nodded decisively. His voice began to shake as he said, "Yes, sir. It was her."

Rudra's brow furrowed. "You mentioned that you saw someone running after the girl. Did you find out who? Was it a man or a woman?"

He hesitated, his eyes darting to the floor as if he were searching for a memory. "No, sir," he admitted, his voice softer now. "By the time I called the police and got closer, she was already pulling the knife out of the girl's body."

Rudra clamped his jaw shut, weighed down by the pressure of it all. Steeling himself, he took a deep breath in. Then, as steadily as possible, began talking again. "Stay here for now. Policeman?"—Rudra turned around towards the policeman in uniform standing next to him.

Satisfied, Rudra turned and walked with purpose towards the interrogation room. His mind raced, piecing together fragments of the story, but the full picture remained elusive. He needed answers—and he intended to get them.

Inside the interrogation room, the air was thick with the weight of silence. The plain metal table stood centre stage, its surface cold and unyielding beneath the overhead light. Durga was seated on one side, hands clasped over a glass of water so fiercely that her knuckles had turned white. Her expression stayed between defiance and fear, looking up at him only for a fleeting second as Rudra stepped inside.

Khaleel, who stood beside the table, straightened when he saw Rudra coming towards him. Wordlessly, Rudra sat down in front of Durga, his movements slow and calculated. Khaleel remained standing beside him, his presence imposing. At the corner of the room, a lady officer had her back against the wall, arms crossed. She seemed to be following the scene that unfolded with a neutral face, her silence emphasising the gravity of the situation.

Rudra broke the silence, his tone firm but measured. "What were you doing near the crime scene?"

Khaleel cut him off before Durga could respond with a sharper voice: "Yeah, and why didn't you report to the police earlier?"

Durga slightly winced at this accusation, her hands shaking as she set the glass of water on the table. Her voice was trembling yet clear as she replied, "I was just trying to learn more about the murders. I thought maybe I could help them."

Rudra's expression deepened. His low voice still carried unmistakable authority as he leaned forward. "Help? By snooping around like some sort of detective? That is certainly not your job, Durga."

Her eyes flashed with defensiveness as she sat upright. "I am a journalist," she countered, her voice gaining strength. "It *is* my job to uncover the truth."

Rudra didn't bat an eyelid. "And you think the best way to do that is by putting yourself in danger? You could have called one of us."

Durga's defiance wavered a little as she looked down. "I tried, I tried calling you, but your phone was unavailable."

Rudra let out a deep breath, running a hand over his hair. Frustration jolted through him. Before he could respond, Durga's voice softened, the words laced with desperation. "I was only trying to help, Rudra."

Her words hung in the air, but Rudra's focus was already shifting as he pieced together what she had seen. Her account, incomplete as it was, painted a vivid picture.

In her mind, Durga replayed the scene so clearly as if it were happening again. The night was filled only by the quiet hum of her bike going over a deserted road. Cool air brushed against her face, and she had been heading home, having drifted off into thought when something caught her eye—a running figure in the distance, frantic.

The woman looked over her shoulder several times. Her gait was jerky and panicky as she ran. Durga slowed down her bike, her brow furrowing as she realised that the woman was being followed. A man in dark clothing closed in behind her with long strides, aggressive.

She was driving, Durga's voice says while describing the scene and how it had occurred, "I saw her running, frightened. And behind her, a man was chasing her."

Durga barely had time to process what was happening when instinct and quick reflexes took over. She followed, her heart racing with every struggling attempt at trying to make sense of the chaos. She hadn't even caught her breath when the woman slipped and fell.

Durga's fingers locked around the handlebars of her bike. Adrenaline burst down her spine. She didn't have to think; she simply responded, screaming out as hard as she could. But it was lost in the quiet of the night, consumed by the distance between her and the tragedy unfolding.

The scene dissolved, pulling Durga back to the present. She looked across the table at Rudra, staring with haunted eyes at the memory still etched on her face. He studied her silently, his expression unreadable as he processed her words.

"Durga," he said finally, his voice softer now but still firm. "You shouldn't have gone there alone. Whatever you saw, it's dangerous."

Her lips quivered, but she remained silent. The image lingered, vivid and relentless. She recognised he was right, but at the moment all she could think about was the fearful face of that woman and the shadowy figure.

Her thoughts slipped back and took her to the dreadful night once again, away from reality. The roar of Durga's bike echoed off the skeletal walls of the under-construction building as she rode in without hesitation. The faint silhouette of the woman, illuminated by the flickering light from a nearby streetlamp, darted deeper into the shadows of the incomplete structure.

Durga's heart pounded in her chest as she slammed on the brakes, and the bike skidded to a halt. Her pulse throbbed in her ears. She jumped off the bike, her feet crunching gravel and broken pieces of concrete on the ground. The air inside the building felt oppressive, thick with dust and the metallic tang of exposed iron rods.

"I don't know what made me follow her," Durga's thoughts ran wild, her inner voice trembling with urgency. "But I did. I couldn't just leave her."

Durga remembered her breathing was ragged as she reached into her pocket, fumbling for her phone. With shaking fingers, she unlocked it and quickly dialled Rudra's number. Each ring was an eternity, a lifeline she desperately needed to hear on the other end of the call.

"Pick up, Rudra," she muttered to herself as she paced anxiously. But the call remained unanswered. She tried again, her thumb hitting redial almost instinctively. The result was the same: silence, except for the mechanical tone of an unreachable line.

Panic seized her chest, but she could not let the fear seize her. Her eyes drifted towards the deeper shadows of the building where the woman had slid into obscurity. Swallowing her fear, she gritted her teeth and moved forward.

"When you didn't pick up," Durga's voice trembled in the present, her recounting vivid in her mind, "I ran to her. I couldn't waste time waiting for help."

—◦◦◦—

She grasps the glass of water with shaking hands, her voice cracking as a tremendous weight threatens to crush her. "But by the time I reached inside," she added, tears running down her face, "the girl was dead."

Her words hung in the air, heavy and chilling. A tear slid down her cheek, tracing a line of anguish across the contours of her face. Rudra sat opposite her, his austere face relaxing. He did not say a word. He reached into his pocket and pulled out a handkerchief to offer her.

Durga hesitated for a moment and took it, holding it shakily. She dabbed her eyes with the handkerchief, blotting her sorrow away.

The following morning, the police station was no less grave. Sunlight streamed through grimy windows, casting half-respectful rays across the busy space of the police station. The door creaked, and an old man entered, his back somewhat stooped but his face stable, walking into the police station with a small girl clutching his hand who was not more than ten years old. The girl clutched him nervously, her eyes wide with unfamiliarity as they darted about the unsettling surroundings.

At the entrance, a stout man with a neatly trimmed moustache had paused when he spotted the pair. He approached them with a polite nod.

"Please tell me, sir," the constable said, his voice carrying the practiced patience of someone accustomed to handling distressed visitors.

The old man cleared his throat and slightly tightened his grip on the girl's hand. "Sir, I want to file a missing person's complaint."

The constable gestured to another officer seated at a desk a few feet away, poring over papers. "Over there," he said. "Constable Ali will help you."

The man nodded his thanks, muttering something softly to the girl as they walked over to the desk. Constable Ali looked up and saw them, furrowing his brow a little at the sight of the nervous child. He gestured towards the chairs in front of his desk. "Please, sit," he said.

The old man sat the girl on the chair and then settled beside her. Ali leaned forward a little, his pen poised over a notepad. "Now, tell me,"He said, his voice businesslike yet not unkind. "Who's missing, and since when?"

He straightened himself up, his voice firm but tinged with concern. "Her name is Kritika," he started off. "She's my neighbour, and she's been missing since last night. This is her daughter."

Ali glanced towards the girl, who shifted back under his gaze. He softened his tone as he asked, "Where is the father of the girl? Why didn't he appear here to lodge this complaint?"

The old man sighed, a weary sound that spoke of long nights and endless worry. "He's out of the country for work," he explained. "I've informed him. He'll be back by tomorrow night."

Ali raised an eyebrow, scepticism creeping into his expression. "Tomorrow?" he asked, his tone incredulous. "His wife is missing, and he can't come sooner?"

The old man shifted with faint displeasure at the accusation. "Sir," he said firmly, "as I said, he is away from the country. I let him know right away. He is in London."

Ali appeared to think over this bit for some time. His pen tapped softly against the desk before nodding.

"Okay," he said. "Do you have a photograph of Kritika?"

The old man reached into his shirt pocket and pulled out a small, slightly creased photograph. He handed it to Ali, his hand rather quivering at the action. Ali took it, studying the image intently before setting it down on the desk. The girl glanced at the photo, her lip trembling as she hugged herself tightly.

The old man gave a gentle, comforting touch to her shoulder. "Don't worry, child," he whispered, "we will find your mother."

Constable Ali reached out, taking the photograph from Pratap Rao's slightly trembling hands. The picture was small, slightly worn at the edges, and bore the image of a woman whose kind eyes seemed to hold an unspoken story. Ali examined it for a brief moment before looking up.

"Please hold on," he said, his tone clipped but polite. Without waiting for a response, he turned on his heel and hurried towards the interrogation room.

Durga sat across from Rudra, her expression a mix of anxiety and frustration, her hands still clutching the handkerchief he had given her earlier. The tension in the room was palpable, each unspoken word adding to the weight of the silence. Khaleel and a female officer stood nearby, their postures stiff as they watched the exchange with subtle concern.

The door creaked open, drawing all eyes to Constable Ali as he stepped inside, his face marked with urgency.

"Sir," Ali said, addressing Rudra directly, "there's a man outside with a little girl. He says the girl's mother has gone missing."

Rudra exchanged a quick, knowing glance with Ali, his sharp instincts immediately alert. Khaleel's brow furrowed as he mirrored Rudra's reaction. Without wasting another second, the three officers exited the room, leaving Durga and the female officer behind.

The door clicked shut, and Durga's gaze instinctively followed the sound, her thoughts racing.

Outside, the police station buzzed with subdued activity. Rudra and Khaleel followed Ali through the thrumming space, the sound of murmured voices and the shuffle of paperwork filling the air. As they reached Ali's desk, Rudra opened his mouth to speak, but the words never came.

The door to the station swung open, and a man in his sixties stepped inside. His movements were deliberate, almost solemn, as he carried a box in his hands. It was small, but its presence commanded immediate attention. Across its lid, smeared in red, was the word "KAALI," glaringly vivid and sinister.

The atmosphere in the station shifted instantly. Conversations stopped mid-sentence. Officers froze, their heads snapping toward the man and the ominous box he held. In a synchronised motion, the officers closest to him reached for their guns, surrounding him in a defensive formation. The tension was electric, crackling through the air like a live wire.

The little girl standing beside Pratap Rao clutched his arm tightly, her face pale and her small body trembling. Sensing her fear, Pratap gently placed a hand over her eyes, shielding her from the chaos unfolding around them. His expression remained steady, though his jaw clenched in visible apprehension.

The room buzzed with unspoken questions, each officer's eyes darting between the box and the man who held it.

Durga stepped out of the interrogation room; her movements tentative. The female officer walked just behind her, her presence a subtle nudge of reassurance. The station was a world away from the small, contained bubble of the interrogation room, and Durga couldn't help but feel an overwhelming sense of disorientation as her eyes adjusted to the broader space.

Her gaze flitted across the room, taking in the flurry of activity and the palpable tension that hung in the air. Then she saw them—Rudra, standing a few paces ahead, his broad shoulders stiff with authority, and Anvi's grandmother with a warmth in her expression that seemed at odds with the chaos around them.

Durga's breath hitched slightly as Anvi's grandmother turned to her, her face softening further into a tender smile. She took a small step forward, her arms extending in a gesture of invitation.

"Come, Durga," Anvi's grandmother said, her voice rich with affection and familiarity. "Let's go home."

Durga's eyes filled with tears as she moved towards her, the relief washing over her like a breaking wave. She stepped into the woman's embrace, her arms wrapping tightly around her as though clinging to a lifeline. The hug was warm, grounding, and everything Durga hadn't realised she needed in that moment.

Rudra watched the scene silently, his usual stern expression softening as he spoke. "Durga," he said, his voice steady but kind, "please go with her to the house. You'll be safe there."

Durga hesitated for the briefest of moments, her gaze meeting Rudra's. There was an unspoken understanding in his eyes, a quiet assurance that this was the right thing to do. She nodded silently, stepping back from the embrace and wiping at her tear-streaked face.

The elderly woman placed a comforting hand on Durga's shoulder, guiding her gently towards the exit. Together, they began to walk away, the chaos of the station fading behind them with each step. Though Durga's heart still carried the weight of the day's events, the warmth of the grandmother's presence brought with it a fragile sense of hope.

And for the first time in what felt like hours, Durga allowed herself to breathe.

Rudra stood outside the interrogation room; his wide shoulders tensed with barely suppressed tension. His dark eyes did not wander from the opaque glass window of the room, where Khaleel questioned the suspect. Every muscle in Rudra's body seemed coiled up, ready to spring, as he waited with a patience that felt like it was teetering on the edge of a knife.

Inside the room, Khaleel sat across from the suspect, staring through him as he fidgeted in his chair. The suspect's eyes, darting everywhere except to where Khaleel bore into them, seemed like he was trying not to lose his grip on the edge of the table. The tiny, antiseptic room felt cramped - the tension was so thick it was a blade waiting to be slashed through.

Khaleel put forward. His voice was calm but firm. "Now tell me, why did you commit the murders?"

The suspect's head jerked up slightly at the accusation, his face a mask of poorly disguised fear. His voice wavered as he replied, "I don't know anything. If I had done something, do you think I would have just walked into the station? I don't even know what's in that box. I saw blood covering it and brought it here."

Khaleel's eyes narrowed, his lips pressing into a thin line. "Stop lying," he said harshly. "If you didn't do it, then tell me who did."

"I am not lying, sir," the suspect protested, his voice trembling. "I swear, I'm telling you the truth."

Outside the interrogation room, Rudra's patience snapped like a brittle thread. No hesitation was needed; he simply pushed open the door and stepped inside, his strides purposeful and laced with barely restrained fury. Khaleel looked up, startled, as Rudra strode across the room in long strides and grabbed the suspect by the collar.

Rudra slammed him against the wall with a force that made the plaster vibrate. Before the man could react or say a word, the suspect let out a panicked gasp, his eyes wide with terror. Rudra pressed his gun firmly into the waistband of the man's pants; his face was but an inch from the suspect's.

"Talk," Rudra growled menacingly. "Or I won't hesitate to end this right now."

The suspect gasped in short, shallow bursts, his body shuddering visibly. A droplet of sweat rolled down his temple as he stammered incoherently, fear temporarily silencing him.

"Sir! Please, sir!" Khaleel's voice cut through the tension as he charged toward Rudra, hands raised in a gesture of placation. "Sir, let's deal with this another way."

Rudra's piercing gaze shifted to Khaleel for a brief moment, his expression unyielding. Khaleel hesitated, recognising the fiery determination in Rudra's eyes, and took a cautious step back.

Turning his attention back to the suspect, Rudra's grip tightened on the man's collar. "Start talking," he demanded, his voice a cold snarl.

The suspect's lips quivered as he finally choked out, "Okay… okay, I'll talk."

Rudra released him abruptly, allowing the man to stumble backwards into his chair. The suspect reached up for his throat, his breaths still light and jagged, rubbing at the place where Rudra's grip had been. He avoided Rudra's piercing gaze, his posture slumping as if the fight had been drained from him.

He settled down across from him, resting his elbows on the table, leaning forward. His eyes never once left the suspect's face, their hard points cutting clearly through the man's brittle composure. "Now tell me," Rudra said evenly, his voice laced with dangerous calm, "why did you kill these people?"

The suspect shifted uncomfortably, his fingers drumming on the table as he avoided eye contact. A small, mocking smile tugged at the corners of his lips. "I like to kill," he said finally, his voice tinged with bitter sarcasm. "It gives me pleasure."

Rudra's eyes narrowed; his jaw tightened. "Pleasure?" he repeated, his tone low and warning. "Tell me the real reason."

The suspect's smile grew wider and turned into something more sinister. "Did you even try to find out," he sneered, dripping mockery, "what they did to deserve this? I'm sure you didn't."

Rudra's patience was wearing thin. He slapped his fist on the table and made the suspect jump. "Cut the crap," he barked. "First, take us to the crime scene."

...✍

Chapter 6

The Aftermath

A police car convoy wove through crowded streets with sirens off, but their presence was unmistakable. The rhythmic hum of engines filled the air as they navigated through the bustling chaos of the city. Khaleel sat in the lead driver's seat in one of those vehicles, eyes firmly fixed on the road ahead. He would glance into the rearview mirror from time to time, checking the cars behind them and the passenger in the rear seat.

Rudra sat beside him in the front passenger seat. His face was stone. The lines underneath the harsh daylight were sharper, his jaw set tight with determination. He was a man on a mission, nothing else going to stand in his way. Shackled in the back seat, the suspect sat with his wrists locked in painful handcuffs. His eyes darted nervously between Rudra and Khaleel, then out at the passing scenery. The man shifted uneasily, his breathing picking up, as the bustle of the city subsided into the outskirts.

Beside the suspect, Constable Ali kept a watchful eye, his hand relaxed on his holstered gun. His presence was a silently whispered warning that any sudden move on his part would be met with swift action. He moved off the main road onto a narrow side road, and his nervousness climbed visibly. His eyes widened as the dense forest loomed ahead; it devoured the car turning onto the narrower path. The sun dimmed under the canopy of trees; the car jolted slightly as it navigated uneven terrain. But it cut off suddenly, the engine letting out a very quiet idle. The four men held their breath for a moment, the suspect's heavy breathing being the sole sound breaking the cool, quiet stillness.

Rudra and Khaleel exchanged a look, though no words passed between them. Rudra pushed open the door silently and stepped out, boots crunching on the dried leaves blanketing the forest floor underfoot. The others trailed, every pace deliberate as they scoped the site. He hesitated, cuffed hands making it awkward to move, but Ali propelled him ahead by his arm. The forest was eerily silent, apart from the occasional rustling in the breeze.

The further in they went, the heavier the air seemed to grow, a grimly foreboding portent hanging over them. And then, as if the trees themselves swept apart to reveal the gruesome truth, they stumbled on the horrifying sight. There were two bodies, sprawled upon the ground, lifeless and twisted in unnatural poses. The wounds were the same pattern as the other murders - the very methodical brutality that had followed them for weeks. He stood frozen, one hand instinctively covering his mouth to stifle a gasp.

Rudra stepped forward, his face settling into the hard lines of his features as he scrutinised everything in sight. Every detail fell into place, piecing together the gruesome puzzle of this horrific case. Besides him, Khaleel saw a glint of metal. He stooped and picked up a purse, its contents partially strewn from the impact of the fall. He straightened and passed it to Rudra, who had already slid on a pair of gloves. Rudra opened the purse with that practiced precision, digging through its contents, searching for something, until he came to a side pocket where an ID card was tucked in. The photograph stared back at him - a smiling woman whose name he didn't need to say aloud. Before he could open his mouth, Ali came closer and peered over Rudra's shoulder.

"Sir," Ali said, his voice tight, "this is the same woman whose neighbour, Pratap Rao, filed a missing person's report this morning."

Rudra's gaze lingered on the ID, his mind racing. He turned to Ali, his voice curt. "Call Pratap Rao and inform him."

Ali nodded briskly. "I'll do that, sir." He stepped away, already pulling out his phone to make the call.

Rudra looked towards Khaleel. "Can we get the forensic team here? They should be here now."

"Yes, sir," Khaleel said, then stepped aside as he pulled out his phone to make all the right calls: for an ambulance and for the forensic team. The voice sounded swallowed by the forest, with grim urgency in every word.

As they waited, the scene around them became heavier, the weight of death settling over the clearing. Rudra's sharp eyes scanned the area again and pieced together broken fragments of information. The bodies, the purse, the suspect's behaviour: it was all part of a larger, more sinister narrative.

The camera pulls back from the dense forest scene, and the fading is but a blip in a profoundly silent night.

———

Rudra entered his own home, the warm dining room a sudden welcome contrast to the chilling sights of the day. The air inside was still, a solemn hush that reflected his mood. Anvi and her grandmother looked up at him as he entered, their faces a mixture of worry and relief.

"Where is Durga?" Rudra asked, his voice steady but laced with concern. "And how is she?"

The grandmother sighed deeply, looking worried. "She is still in a state of shock," she replied. "She hasn't stepped out of her room since we arrived. I called her for both lunch and dinner, but she just doesn't want to eat. She's barely spoken a word."

Her words hung in the air, a concrete reminder of the emotional toll this ordeal had taken on their family. "Why don't you go see her?" the grandmother added after a moment. "Maybe she will listen to you."

Nodding, Rudra's jaw clamped together as he turned and walked down the hall to Durga's room. Every step became heavier than the one before it; the weight of the day's horrors mixed with the dread that was building inside at what he might see in his loved one. He paused in front of her door, hesitating, hand lifting to knock. The sound carried faintly in the otherwise silent house, but there came no response from the other side.

He stood there for a moment, then rapped again, more forcefully this time. Still nothing. He took a deep breath and went for the handle, then pushed open the door and stepped inside.

Bedroom darkness was heavy with shadows, only illuminated enough by a nightlight's faint glow to cast soft, flickering shapes on the walls. Rudra stood in the doorway, the weight of the moment settling heavily on his shoulders. He flipped the switch, and the sudden light reflected the modest simplicity of the room. Durga sat on the edge of the bed with a closed posture, defeated. Her head dropped down, hair concealing much of her face, shoulders slumping forward as if trying to support an invisible weight. "Durga?" Rudra's voice was soft, almost reluctant, as he came into the room. The fragility that confronted him made him tread gingerly.

She did not utter a word, her silence a thick wall between them. He moved over to the bed and lowered himself onto the edge next to her. The mattress dipped under him, and for a moment, he sat there, his presence an unspoken attempt at comfort.

"I know…" Rudra started, his voice level but laced with self-reproach. "I know what you've been through since last night is tough, but trust me—everything is over now."

Durga's shoulders shook as a sob escaped her lips. She finally lifted her face, streaked with tears, her eyes brimming with pain. "But you didn't believe me," she whispered, her voice trembling. The accusation hung in the air, cutting deeper than she'd ever intended; but it was her truth, raw and unfiltered.

Rudra drew in a deep breath, the enormity of her words hitting him like a blow.

"I know," he admitted, his tone laced with regret. "I didn't believe you, but how could I? You were standing there… with a knife…" His words faltered, and he paused, the memory clearly haunting him as much as it did her. "Look," he said after a moment, his voice softer now, "I am sorry. Truly, I am. But everything will be okay now. I promise you that." He reached out, resting a hesitant hand on her shoulder, but it is Durga who leaned forward for the comfort of his strength. She rested her head-on his shoulder, sobs dripping into his shirt as she sat still, letting him bear the weight of all she felt. Rudra remained unmoving, unsaid: he just let her cry through the tempest of feelings she was fighting.

The following morning, the house was given a different kind of stillness by the air that was lighter, though faint echoes of the past night lingered. Rudra sat on the couch in the living room. The morning sun broke through the windows, casting a warm glow over the room, as he cradled steaming cupfuls of coffee in his hands. He sipped his coffee thoughtfully, the events of the previous day still fresh in his mind.

The creak of the door opened, and he noticed Durga stepping out of the bedroom. She was dressed in a simple blue kurti paired with blue jeans. Her entire attire seemed as understated as she was. Though calmer, there were faint traces of exhaustion on her face. But somehow, that quiet resolve in her eyes had been present in a manner that it hadn't been the previous night.

Rudra smiled as Durga walked into the room, her very presence like a reassuring sign of resilience. "How are you feeling?" he asked, placing his cup on the table. "And where are you going?"

Durga offered him a faint smile in return. "Better now," she replied. "I'm going to the office."

It made Rudra frown a little, for it was instinctively awakened by that fight. "Why don't you take a break for a few days?" he suggested, with a hint of gentleness though firm.

"No, I cannot," Durga shook her head as her spirit refused to bend into submission. "I have to do the report and submit it to the boss. The case is closed."

Do you want me to drop you?" Rudra offered, his concern evident in the way he leaned forward, ready to help at a moment's notice.

"No, no," Durga replied quickly, waving off his suggestion. "I'll go by myself."

Rudra sat back, studying her intently. "At least have something to eat before you go," he urged, not entirely comfortable with letting her leave in her current state.

Before Durga could react, the grandmother emerged from the room, steps deliberate, and countenance furrowed with concern. "Durga, where are you off to?" she asked, a tinge of concern in her voice.

"She's going to work," Rudra replied before Durga could open her mouth. "I was telling her to take a break, but she wanted to get back to work."

The old lady frowned in disapproval. "Why, Durga? Let's all stay in for a few days. You must rest."

Durga smiled warmly at her, her tone polite but resolute. "No, Auntie. I have to complete my work. I'll be back as soon as I'm through."

"But," the grandmother began, but Rudra cut her short.

"Mom," he said gently, "let her go. She needs the diversion."

Durga looked between them; the gratitude of Rudra's understanding evident in her eyes. She walked closer and gave the grandmother a very quick hug. "See you soon," she said softly and moved away towards the door.

The grandmother watched her leave; a sigh escaped her lips as the door clicked shut. "I feel so sorry for Durga," she said, her voice heavy with sadness. "Poor girl has to go through all this."

Rudra leaned back against the couch, his gaze lingering on the door through which Durga had just exited. "I know," he said quietly. "But she'll get through it. She's stronger than we think."

He rose again with his coffee, the heat from the mug anchoring him as he took another sip. However, his mind was elsewhere - with Durga, silently hoping that she would be able to gather the strength of will move ahead from the darkness of her pain.

Durga pulled into the assigned parking with a practiced ease. The familiar hum of the engine died as she turned the key, and the metallic clink of releasing the gears echoed in the otherwise quiet lot. She swung her leg over the seat and smoothly got off the bike, opening the storage compartment. Her helmet was tucked safely in, the click of the latch serving as closure to the small ritual with which she had prepared herself. Steeling herself, she stood up straight, corrected her kurti, slung her bag over her shoulder, and headed into the building.

The elevator ride up was uneventful, the soft hum of machinery punctuated only by the occasional ding of passing floors. Durga entered the brightly lit, bustling lobby of her office as the sliding doors opened. The familiar atmosphere enveloped her like a second skin, while turmoil seemed to remain far behind. Quiet determination moved her as she nodded at smiling colleagues who acknowledged her presence. It was such a day when small gestures meant so much that she drew comfort from those brief, tense interactions.

Her desk, tucked neatly into a corner, was a refuge. She slid herself into the chair, sitting in gentle, almost meditative movement. As she settled back, her elbows hit the surface of the desk, and her head came down into her hands for a moment, resting like a sodden weight against palms loaded with fatigue: physical and emotional both. Yet there was comfort in being here, in routine's very normalcy.

A gentle touch on her shoulder broke her reverie. Durga was startled but not alarmed. She turned to find her friend and colleague standing beside her. The concern in her friend's eyes was palpable, and it softened Durga's expression. She managed a small smile, grateful for the unspoken support.

"I'm so sorry to hear about your situation," her friend said softly, her voice warm and filled with empathy. "I hope everything is fine now."

Durga straightened in her chair, brushing a stray lock of hair behind her ear. "Thank you," she said, her voice steady despite the lingering tremors of recent events. "Everything is fine now."

Her friend hesitated, studying her closely as if searching for cracks beneath this composed exterior. "But why did you come in today?" she asked gently. "You should have taken a couple of days off."

Durga shook her head lightly. The movement was deliberate. "I needed to finish the article about the case," she explained. "And honestly, I just wanted to get out of the house for a bit."

There was a silence between them; her friend nodded understandingly. "Well," she said after a moment, "call me if you need to."

"I will," she said, smiling faintly at that, her voice neutral. When her friend departed, Durga turned to her own desk. She switched on her monitor, the screen glowing to life. The computer bloomed quietly into a murmur, that gentle whir the machine always seemed to make, so familiar and almost reassuring. Taking a deep breath, the tension ebbed from her shoulders as her attention turned once again to the task in hand.

In the Commissioner's office, there was already a press conference in full swing. The room was abuzz with huddled media people chatting softly, punctuated by the rustling of papers and recording devices humming in the background. A long desk dominated the front of the room, behind which Commissioner Krishna Reddy, Rudra, and Khaleel sat with solemnly composed expressions.

Krishna Reddy, towering and authoritative, sat at the centre. Seated at his right was Rudra, a face that was professional in itself but had a small worn-out look of exhaustion, for the weight of the case said much for his body language. Khaleel sat at the Commissioner's left, his sharp gaze scanning through the room, always prepared to pounce. Stood off to one side, gazing steadfastly forward, was Constable Ali, a witness more to silence and seriousness than to anything else.

The Commissioner leaned forward, speaking calmly and precisely. "Good afternoon," he started, his deep voice piercing through the ambient noise. "As you all know, over the past few months, we've had trouble pinpointing who the murderer is, responsible for these heinous crimes."

A journalist in the front row, notepad in hand, raised his voice to ask the question on everyone's mind. "Commissioner, can you provide us with an update on the investigation?"

Krishna Reddy gazed briefly at Rudra and Khaleel before speaking. "Our team has strived hard to bring justice to the victims and their families. Officer Rudra, with Officer Khaleel, has led this investigation"

Words spoken at the desk resounded through the room as the press conference went on; evidence of the painstaking work and unwavering commitment that brought someone to this very moment. Every soul there - whether a police officer or a journalist -

felt the weight of this story told, one that would echo for miles beyond the confines of this room.

Durga's boss flung open the cabin door with an abrupt movement of his tall frame, silhouetted against the bright light spilling in from the large windows behind him. His face was calm yet commanding, his tone strong with the weight of someone who could be counted upon to be obeyed without question.

"Come, Durga," he said, his voice firm but not unkind.

Seated at her desk, Durga lifted her head and looked in his direction. She blinked, then shook her head, as if to snap herself awake from the thoughts she had temporarily drifted off into while typing away on the article. She nodded afterwards, acknowledging.

"Please come," he said, stepping away to clear a path for her.

Durga stood, smoothing out the fabric of her kurti, and walked towards the cabin with purposeful strides. Her mind buzzed with curiosity; he rarely summoned her unless something critical was afoot. As she stepped into the room, the familiar scent of leather and paper filled her nostrils. Her boss gestured towards the television mounted on the wall, its screen aglow with a live broadcast.

"Look at this," he said, pointing a finger at the screen.

Durga followed the gesture with a slight wrinkling of her eyes, taking in the scene. The image on the screen is of Rudra sitting at the press conference to address the reporters. The camera zooms in closer, his face enlarged, every nuance of his expression broadcast clearly, sharp as a pin.

The room was silent except for the soft glow of the TV. Durga's heartbeat accelerated because she could sense the intensity of Rudra's behaviour. She sat in her chair opposite her boss, staring intently at the unfolding press conference.

—◆—

At the Commissioner's office, the press conference was in full swing - the room crackled with the energy of unrelenting journalists, whose pens were poised and cameras flashed intermittently. Rudra sat behind the desk with a calm and composed posture. His uniform was impeccable, the brass buttons catching the light, lending him the authority that matched the gravity of the situation.

A journalist in the front row leans forward, her voice carrying over the din of the room. "Rudra, Sir, do you believe the killer had a reason for giving himself up?"

Rudra looked at her, his face steady but with a flicker of thoughtfulness as he considered the response. "I think he surrendered so that he could make a statement," Rudra said, his tone firm and deliberate. "He showed the world that he is smarter than the police. That we could not take him."

There was a brief pause as the journalists scribbled furiously, filled with the scratch of pens on notepads. Another journalist raised his hand and spoke quickly, almost without waiting to be acknowledged. "So, you and your team didn't actually find the killer?"

Rudra's jaw clenched for a split second before he said anything, his voice steady but firm. "We did everything we could," he said, scanning the room. "But one thing my team and I knew is that he had a desire to receive recognition. He was hungry for the limelight, and we were not going to give it to him."

His words lingered in the room for a minute, the heaviness of his conviction palpable. The room seemed to collectively lean in, every ear open to everything he had to say.

Another journalist, braver than the rest, interjected with a note of scepticism in his voice. "Do you actually believe that withholding fame forced him to surrender?"

"Yes," said Rudra, unflinching, his voice steady. "When we saw that video he made, it was pretty obvious he wanted attention for himself. He sought people to know who he was and what he could do. Never showing him, that attention locked his hand."

The journalists looked at one another, murmurs circulating through the crowd as they digested his explanation. One voice rose above the din. "Did he say why he committed the crimes?"

Rudra paused for a moment before answering, his expression turning sombre. "Not yet. But he soon will."

Pratap Rao sat on the plush, dark leather couch, his fingers interlocked in front of him, exuding an air of both authority and weariness. His expression was a guarded mask, but his sharp eyes betrayed a hint of unease. Across from him, Rudra and Khaleel sat side by side on the opposing couch, their postures alert yet composed. The tension in the room was palpable, the silence punctuated by the occasional muffled sounds of movement as the assistant cops, along with Constable Ali, searched the other rooms for clues. There, near the corner of the room, stood quietly a girl no more than ten years of age with wide, fearful, and confused eyes. She clutched at a maid almost sixty years of age, whose wrinkled face was deeply set into concern. The small hands of the girl clutched the folds of the saree at the maid's waist for comfort.

He looked around, his face relaxing a little as his attention settled on the maid. "Take her inside, please," he asked softly, his voice measured and almost gentle, as if in keeping with the rest of his manner, afraid to upset the child further.

The maid nodded to herself and moved quietly, ushering the girl into one of the bedrooms. The girl stopped for a moment, taking in the occupants of the room with wide questioning eyes before being swept from view down the hallway.

Rudra turned his attention back to Pratap Rao, his tone reining back into one of professional resolve. He reached into his pocket and produced a small plastic evidence bag. Inside was a badge, its insignia reflected in the dim light of the living room.

"Sir," Rudra started, his voice steady but infused with an undertone of intensity. "We found this badge next to a dead body this morning."

Pratap Rao stiffened visibly, his composure momentarily cracking as shock flickered across his face. He leaned forward slightly, his brows knitting together in disbelief. "What are you saying?" he murmured, his voice barely above a whisper.

Rudra did not break eye contact, choosing each word cautiously. "I am still not sure if it is the same person," he admitted, his tone professional yet weighted with caution. "The forensic team is still running tests to confirm the DNA."

Pratap Rao exhaled slowly and fell onto the sofa, trying to gather his head around the possibility. Rudra's words pressed down on him like a heavy weight, and the stillness in the room seemed all the more oppressive.

"If it's true…" Pratap Rao had started to say, but a shiver ran through his voice before he could steady himself. "Why would someone do this to her?" His eyes sought out Rudra's face as if he expected some explanation that would make it all meaningful.

There was no time for Rudra to say a word.

Everybody in the room looked towards the door as Naresh, Kritika's husband, entered. He was still in his formal office attire, with the weariness of the day reflected in his dishevelled appearance. In one hand, he gripped his laptop bag and pulled out a small suitcase using his other hand, rushing and distracted.

Naresh hardly noticed who was in the room as he opened his laptop bag and set it beside the suitcase, entirely concentrated. His voice echoed out into the room, urgent and quivering. "Urmila!" he cried, his tone edged with desperation. "Urmila… where are you?"

The name seemed to hang in the air like a shard of glass, cutting through the tension with its stark clarity.

Urmila was seated on the edge of the bed, clutching her small stuffed bunny close to her chest. The soft murmur of voices from the living room filtered into the bedroom, muffled yet heavy with tension. But then, a familiar voice rose above it all, cutting through her fear and confusion like a beacon. It was her father.

"Papa!" she gasped, her voice trembling as tears welled in her eyes. She dropped the bunny without a second thought and darted towards the door, her small feet padding swiftly across the cold floor. She flung the door open and ran into the hallway, her sobs now audible.

In the living room, Naresh had barely settled his suitcase and laptop bag down when he saw her. He dropped to one knee, arms wide open just in time to catch his daughter as she threw herself into his embrace. Her little arms clung tightly around his neck as her body trembled against his.

"I'm here now," Naresh murmured, his voice low but firm as he tried to soothe her. He stroked her hair gently, his touch tender despite the chaos brewing around them. "Everything will be fine, beta. I promise."

Rudra, who had been observing the scene silently, stood up from the couch and walked over to Naresh. His calm yet authoritative demeanour cast a steadying presence over the room. Clearing his throat slightly to draw Naresh's attention, Rudra spoke.

"Mr. Naresh," Rudra said, his voice even but laced with purpose, "I am sorry to hear about your wife and would like to speak to you about it."

Naresh pulled back slightly from Urmila; his face tight with worry. "Of course, Officer," he replied, his tone subdued but cooperative. "What would you like to know?"

Naresh glanced down at Urmila, gently patting her back to calm her. "Go back to your room, beta," he said softly. "Papa will come to see you in a little while."

Reluctantly, Urmila obeyed, wiping her tears with the back of her hand as she shuffled back to the bedroom. Once she was out of sight, Naresh walked over to the dining table and sat down heavily in one of the chairs. His elbows rested on the table, and his hands came up to press against his forehead, as though bracing himself for what was to come.

Rudra followed, pulling out a chair across from him and sitting down. His eyes stayed fixed on Naresh, assessing him carefully. "How long have you been away?" Rudra asked, his tone professional and direct.

Naresh let out a long breath before replying. "It's been a few days. As soon as I heard she was missing, I took the earliest flight back," he said, his voice tinged with exhaustion and grief.

Rudra leaned back slightly in his chair; his gaze unwavering. "What is it that you do for a living?" he asked.

"I work as the head of sales and marketing for Nimbus Innovation," Naresh replied. "My job keeps me travelling across India, Europe, and Asia. It's demanding, but…" His voice trailed off as he gestured helplessly, his words implying that his work had taken him away from his family more often than he liked.

"May I see your passport and ticket?" Rudra asked, his tone still neutral, though there was an edge of formality that made it clear this was not just a routine question.

"Of course," Naresh said without hesitation. He stood up, walked over to his laptop bag, and retrieved the items Rudra requested. Returning to the table, he handed them over with steady hands, though his eyes betrayed a flicker of nervousness.

Rudra took the documents and carefully flipped through the passport, scrutinising the stamps and dates. He then examined the ticket, cross-referencing it with the information. Satisfied for the moment, he set them aside and leaned forward slightly.

"Do you know of anyone who might have a grudge against you or your family?" Rudra asked, his tone probing yet calm.

Naresh shook his head firmly. "No, sir," he replied. "As far as I know, we've never had any enemies or conflicts that would lead to something like this."

"And what about your wife?" Rudra continued. "What did she do? Any professional or personal connections that might raise questions?"

Naresh's face softened at the mention of Kritika. "She was a homemaker," he said. "Her life revolved around our family, especially Urmila. She loved her... loved us... more than anything."

Rudra's expression remained unreadable as he pressed on. "Are you sure about that?" he asked pointedly. "Because her body was found with another man."

The statement hung in the air like a weight, causing Naresh's jaw to tighten. He blinked rapidly, his hands clenching into fists on the table. "What do you mean, Officer?" he demanded, his voice rising slightly. "Which man?"

Rudra gestured towards Khaleel, who had been standing silently by. Khaleel stepped forward and handed Rudra a photograph encased in a clear evidence bag. Rudra placed it on the table in front of Naresh, pushing it towards him.

"Do you recognise him?" Rudra asked, his voice steady.

Naresh stared at the image, his brow furrowing as he examined the face of the man in the photograph. After a few moments, he shook his head firmly. "No," he said, his voice resolute. "I've never seen this man before in my life."

Rudra's gaze didn't waver. "So, you don't suspect anyone? Not even a possibility of someone holding a grudge or acting out of revenge?"

"No, Officer," Naresh replied, his tone now tinged with frustration. "I can't think of anyone who would want to hurt her. She was a good person. She didn't deserve this."

Rudra regarded him for a long moment before nodding slightly. He stood up, signalling the end of their conversation for the time being. "I'd like to speak to your maid now," he said, his voice calm but firm.

Naresh got up as well, his movements mechanical as though he were running on autopilot. He walked to the bedroom where the maid had been staying. Knocking lightly on the door, he said, "The officer wants to speak to you. Please come out."

The maid emerged a moment later, her expression apprehensive but composed. She walked to the dining table and took a seat, folding her hands nervously in her lap. Rudra sat back down across from her, his gaze steady.

"How long have you been working in this house?" Rudra asked, his tone gentle but purposeful.

"About a year, sir," the maid replied, her voice quiet but clear.

"And how was Kritika as a mother and wife?" Rudra continued, leaning forward slightly to catch her answer.

The maid's face softened at the question. "She was a wonderful person, sir," she said earnestly. "She made sure Urmila had everything she needed. She loved her daughter so much... more than anything in the world."

"And Naresh?" Rudra asked, his tone neutral but probing.

The maid hesitated for a fraction of a second, her eyes flickering briefly toward Naresh before returning to Rudra. "Him also," she replied, though her tone carried a faint note of reservation.

Rudra didn't miss the subtle shift in her demeanour, but he didn't press her immediately. "Did you notice anything unusual in the last few days?" he asked instead. "Anything at all?"

"No, sir," the maid replied, shaking her head. "She seemed happy. There was nothing out of the ordinary."

Rudra studied her for a moment, his eyes narrowing slightly as though searching for any hint of hesitation or omission. Finally, he nodded. "If you remember anything—anything at all, no matter how small—please let us know," he said firmly.

The maid nodded quickly. "Yes, sir," she said. "I will."

Satisfied for now, Rudra leaned back in his chair, the wheels in his mind already turning as he pieced together the fragments of information.

Chapter 7

The Race Against Time

Rudra pushed his hand towards the door and steadied himself at the doorway to Kritika's room, the silver doorknob beneath his hand. His breath was shallow as he steeled himself inwardly to turn it over and allow the faint luminescence that poured over him to brighten the subtle perfume scent in the dim room, faintly lit by partially opened curtains and throwing thin stripes across the floor.

Stepping in, Rudra's sharp gaze started methodically sweeping the room. The bed was perfect; its soft floral comforter was carefully smoothed out, and the pillows were precision-placed. On the nightstand, a framed photograph attracted his attention. It was a family picture: Kritika, Naresh, and Urmila, all smiling as if frozen in one perfect moment of happiness. Beside it lay an open book. Its pages were creased to indicate that someone had come to a pause mid-sentence.

Rudra approached the dresser, opening the drawers one by one. Each was meticulously organised—rows of neatly folded clothes, carefully arranged jewellery, and personal items stored in small compartments. Nothing seemed out of place, yet the very neatness felt unnaturally deliberate. He moved to the vanity, where an assortment of makeup, brushes, and perfume bottles cluttered the surface. Rudra shifted a few items aside, searching for anything that might hint at a deeper story.

The closet door creaked open slightly. Inside, rows of clothes hung in precise alignment. Rudra ran his fingers over the fabric of a dress, his eyes scanning every corner. The closet looked normal, with no apparent secrets. Still, he had a feeling that he needed to look deeper.

His eyes landed on the desk that rested under the window, with all sorts of scattered papers, notebooks, and a laptop strewn over it. Rudra picked up the laptop and placed it aside, inspecting it closely. Flipping open a notebook, he read its pages swiftly, scanning the lines of handwriting. There were some entries that intrigued him; the tone of which was contemplative but remained inconclusive.

Just as he was leaving the room, something caught his eye. It was a small box partially tucked beneath the bed. Rudra got on his haunches, carefully taking it out. He opened the lid to find letters and photographs inside. The photographs depicted Kritika with a man who was obviously not Naresh. The letters were passionate, written in a flowing hand that hinted at an intense emotional connection. A knot tightened in Rudra's chest—this could be the lead he was looking for.

Striding forward, Rudra called out, his voice steady but firm. "Maid."

The maid appeared quickly; her footsteps hurried. "Yes, sir?" she asked, her voice trembling slightly as she stood in the doorway.

"Take the girl outside," Rudra instructed, gesturing towards Urmila.

The maid nodded and disappeared, re-emerging in a moment to lead Urmila out of the house. Naresh was standing in the living room, and he entered the bedroom now, his face set with confusion.

"What happened, sir?" Naresh asked, furrowing his brow.

He tossed the photographs and letters onto the bed without any reaction, not even an eyelash flicker. The papers' contents were thrown all about. "You are saying that you do not know a thing about these pictures and letters?" Rudra sounded unconvinced by Naresh's tone.

Naresh stepped closer and began pulling one of the photographs closer. His face lost colour upon scanning its contents. "Sir, I really do not know anything about these," he said with a very low and strangled tone.

Rudra narrowed his eyes. "Naresh, stop lying. You live in this house, you share this bedroom, and still you don't know that your wife was screwing behind your back?"

Naresh sank onto the edge of the bed, his shoulders slumping. He let his head drop into his hands, his voice heavy with resignation. "I recently came to know about this," he said, gesturing towards the photographs. "These pictures and letters... they were before our marriage."

He breathed out deeply, putting the photographs beside him. "We even argued about it," he continued in a nearly inaudible voice. "That's when she told me everything."

—◆—

Flashback

Naresh was sitting on the edge of the bed. The photographs and letters were clutched in his shaking hands. His face full of disbelief mixed with hurt. He heard her opening the door. Her movements were hesitant as she walked into the room.

"Are you alright?" Kritika asked, her voice gentle yet cautious as she moved towards him.

Naresh did not look up at first, but when he did, his eyes locked onto hers with a force that made her freeze. Her eyes darted to the objects in his hands, and she cleared her throat, feeling that something was amiss.

"Naresh," Kritika started, her voice breaking.

Naresh held up one of the photographs, his voice taut with emotion. "What are these?" he demanded, his tone a mix of accusation and confusion.

Kritika hesitated, her eyes darting between Naresh and the incriminating evidence. "These are old pictures and letters," she said, her voice trembling. "It was before our marriage."

"But what are they doing here now?" Naresh's voice rose; his frustration was evident.

Kritika wrung her hands nervously. "I received them in the post the other day," she confessed. "I didn't know what to do with them, so I kept them hidden. I planned to discard them before you found out."

Naresh's jaw tightened. "So you wanted to hide all of this from me?" he asked, his voice bitter.

"It's my past, Naresh," Kritika implored, taking a step forward. "It has nothing to do with my present. Do trust me."

Naresh pushed back his chair, rising decisively. The photographs and letters fell from his hands and scattered across the bed as he strode to pick up his suitcase and laptop bag; he was swift and forceful.

Kritika watched as the words came from his lips, her eyes brimmed with tears. "Naresh, please," she muttered, her voice cracking, but Naresh didn't respond. He slung the bag over his shoulder and paused for a short while, his angry and disappointment-filled gaze met hers and then turned out of that room, leaving Kritika standing amidst the ruins of her life.

Naresh blinked, snapping out of the trance. His eyes shot up to meet Rudra's, now wearied. "That is the truth," he said, his voice low. "She told me everything, and I left that night. Couldn't stay… needed to process all of it."

Rudra looked at him intently, weighing the sincerity in his words. He didn't say a word, giving the weight of Naresh's confession time to settle into the room. The atmosphere was heavy with tension; the questions left unanswered hung there like a storm cloud overhead.

Rudra stood in the dimly lit bedroom, his piercing gaze fixed on Naresh, who was sitting at the edge of the bed. The tension hung in the air like an electric charge, each second stretching endlessly. Naresh's face was deathly pale, his hands slightly trembling as they lay on his knees. The weight of Rudra's accusation hung in the air like an oppressive cloud.

That's why you killed them both," Rudra said sternly, his voice expressionless.

Naresh looked up sharply, his eyes wide with disbelief. "No, Sir!" he exclaimed, his voice cracking. "After the fight, I left Hyderabad for work. I wasn't here. When Pratap Uncle called, I came back immediately. I swear!"

Rudra's piercing eyes did not budge. He took a step closer, towering over Naresh. "Naresh, for now, you are coming with us," he said. His tone was calm but left no room for argument.

Naresh's breath quickened, and he shook his head as if trying to shake off a nightmare. "Sir, I really didn't do anything. Please, you have to believe me. I would never—"

Sorry, Naresh," Rudra interrupted, his voice firm but with a hint of regret.

Naresh's shoulders slumped under the weight of despair, and his face crumpled. "What about my daughter?" he whispered, breaking into tears. His pain was evident in the rivers of tears that streamed down his face.

Rudra took a deep breath and looked away as if to collect himself. "We will tell your family," he said, his voice softer now. But the determination in his words didn't waver.

Naresh wiped his face with his shaking hands and nodded, though his face was a mixture of resignation and sadness. Rudra gestured towards the door. "Can we go?"

Naresh slowly rose from the bed, as if each movement was an uphill battle, taking a laborious step after the other. Giving the room a final wistful glance, with all the memories it contained of his family, he stepped out behind Rudra and Officer Khaleel.

As they entered the living room, the silence was broken by the sound of hurried footsteps. Urmila ran towards her father, her small arms wrapping tightly around his legs. "Dad," she cried, her voice trembling with fear.

Naresh immediately knelt down, pulling her into a tight embrace. "Don't worry, beta," he whispered, stroking her hair gently. "I will be back soon. Be brave for me, okay?"

Tears welled up in Urmila's eyes, but she nodded, holding onto her father as if letting go would mean losing him forever. Rudra watched the scene silently, his jaw tightening. Moments like these were the hardest part of his job.

Pratap approached and placed a reassuring hand on Urmila's shoulder, pulling her into his arms. "I'll take care of her," he said softly, his voice filled with quiet determination. The maid stood nearby, her face a mask of worry as she watched Naresh being led away.

The front door opened, and Rudra, Khaleel, and Naresh stepped into the corridor. Hardly a moment after, they heard murmurs reach their ears. Neighbours had gathered, their curious and judgemental gazes following Naresh's every move as he walked past them, flanked by the officers.

As they reached the parking lot, Rudra looked around, patting his pockets absently. A frown creased his forehead. "Where's my phone?" he muttered to himself.

Officer Khaleel noticed his superior's agitation. "What's wrong, sir?" he asked.

"I think I left my phone in Naresh's apartment," Rudra said, looking up at the building.

"Let me go and get it for you," Khaleel offered.

Rudra shook his head. "No, it's fine. I'll get it myself." Without waiting for a response, he turned and walked briskly towards the elevator, leaving Khaleel and Naresh by the car.

At home in the apartment, the atmosphere felt oppressively quiet. When Rudra entered, his keen senses could pick up a slight sound of movement from the kitchen. He walked towards the kitchen, hearing the silent tiled floor beneath his feet. And with each step, his voice grew clearer.

Inside the kitchen stood the maid, talking quickly into her phone. Her voice was animated, almost celebratory. "They've arrested Naresh," she said, a sigh of relief in her voice. "I am so happy. My husband will finally get out of jail."

Rudra furrowed his brow as he entered the doorway. "Who are you talking to?" he asked, his voice slicing through the maid's conversation like a knife.

Startled, the maid turned abruptly, the phone slipping from her grasp. Her eyes widened in shock as she saw Rudra standing there, his piercing gaze locked on her.

"No one, sir," she stammered, her voice shaky.

Rudra took a step closer, his eyes narrowing. "Don't lie to me," he said sternly. "Tell me the truth, or you'll end up in prison as well."

She wrung her hands nervously before finally breaking under his pressure of gaze. "Sir, the one who surrendered yesterday, he is my husband," she whispered to him barely.

Rudra's eyes popped open in shock. "What?" he exclaimed in disbelief and suspicion.

"Yes, Sir," the maid continued. "Naresh did not even know that Kritika was still seeing her lover."

Rudra's mind racing over what she said, asked him, "Then why wasn't it said the time when I questioned you?"

Tears welled in the maid's eyes as she looked down in shame. "Because I did not want Naresh to know," she whispered. "I didn't want him to come and find out that Kritika was still involved with somebody."

Realisation dawned on Rudra, and his expression darkened. "That means Naresh has nothing to do with the murders?" he asked, his voice low but urgent.

"Yes, Sir," the maid confirmed, nodding emphatically. "He's innocent."

Rudra exhaled sharply, running a hand through his hair. "Oh, God," he muttered under his breath. "But why would your husband do that?"

The maid hesitated, biting her lip. "I can't tell you the reason," she said finally.

Rudra's temper flared. "Have you gone haywire?" he shouted. "He killed innocents. This is something that's kept under the blanket? That's a bloody lie!"

Rudra's phone buzzed in his pocket before the maid could utter a word, interrupting the tense exchange. He pulled it out and answered the call, his demeanour immediately changing to one of urgency. Without another word to the maid, he turned and strode out of the apartment, his mind already racing ahead to the next steps.

In deathly silence, the gravel in the driveway seemed to rustle alive only with the rhythmic chirping of crickets under the dim glow of the streetlights. Only outside the house stood a tautly tensile frame, Anvi's grandmother. Her eyes shot repeatedly to the gate; her face was shadowed with worry. She tightly clutched a paper in her hands, from which the crumpled edges betrayed hours spent embracing it in anticipation.

The quiet was broken by a low hum of an approaching vehicle, and soon enough, Rudra's jeep appeared, cutting through the darkness with its headlights. Gravel crunched under its tyres as it came to a halt in front of her. He didn't even need to get out before the old woman hurried towards him and thrust the paper into his hands.

Please, Rudra," she begged, her voice cracking under the weight of her emotions. "Bring her back.

Rudra gave her a solemn nod, his face a mask of determination. He didn't offer any words of reassurance – he didn't need to. The silent exchange between them was enough. He folded the paper with care, slid it into his pocket, and drove off, the jeep disappearing into the endless stretch of the road as the grandmother stood watching, her figure shrouded in the night's uncertainty.

The city streets stretched out like a labyrinth, empty and shrouded in oppressive stillness. Rudra's knuckles whitened as he gripped the steering wheel hard, the weight of the mission bearing down on him.

Streetlights cast fleeting shadows on his face, their orange glow illuminating the lines of tension etched on his features. The road stretched endlessly before him with every turn of the wheel, bringing him closer and yet no closer. His thoughts were racing right alongside the speeding jeep, a scenario playing out in his head for every possibility. What was unknown gnawed at him, coiled tightly in his chest like a snake. Night, in this way, grew heavier with every passing minute, darkness seeming to conspire to stretch time itself.

Finally, an empty abandoned house stood out before him, its silhouette ominous against the starless sky. Rudra jerked the brakes hard, making the jeep skid to an abrupt stop. The vehicle groaned under his hands as he got out and slammed the door shut behind him. His breath was shallow, gasps, the tension palpable in the frosty night air. It stood silent and foreboding, the darkened mouth of some waiting beast.

Rudra hastened his footsteps towards the house, his hand automatically rubbing against the firearm tucked into his waist. He pushed the door open with a rusty sound, and it echoed in the deserted building. The air inside was oppressive, filled with the minute smell of damp and rot. His eyes scanned around the room until they fixed on a figure slumped in a chair and a man motionless on the floor.

Durga," he breathed, his voice barely above a whisper.

She was bound to the chair, head down, hair dishevelled and streaked with tears on her face. It made his heart ache seeing her bruised and broken form. Rudra went running to her side and knelt before her, lifting her chin. Her eyes fluttered open, heavy with exhaustion and glassy, but brightened a little at seeing him.

"I'm here now," Rudra said softly, his tone steady but laced with emotion. He worked quickly, untying the ropes that bound her wrists and ankles. As the last knot gave way, Durga leaned into him, her weight a testament to her ordeal.

"Stay close," Rudra instructed, his tone firm as he steadied her. Just then, a chilling voice rang out from the shadows, its icy timbre cutting through the room.

"Rudra."

The voice sent a shiver down his spine. He instinctively positioned himself in front of Durga, shielding her.

His hand went to his firearm, and he pulled it free, pointing it in the direction of the voice.

"Show yourself," Rudra commanded, his voice sharp.

A woman slowly materialised from the darkness—a figure in her thirties, dressed head to toe in black. Her jeans and hoodie were indistinguishable from the shadows, but she was not a stealthy figure. In one hand, she gripped another woman, her knife pressed cruelly against the hostage's throat. Bruising covered the woman's face, and her eyes were wide with terror as muffled cries escaped from behind the tape covering her mouth.

"Let her go," Rudra demanded, his voice like a whip crack in the stillness.

Kaali's lips twisted into a grim smile, her eyes burning with a mix of defiance and disdain. "Drop your gun, Rudra, or she dies right here, right now."

Rudra didn't waver. "How can you justify this? Killing innocent people? They had families. They had children."

"Innocent?" Kaali spat, her voice rising with venom. "Those women cared about nothing except their own pleasures. Do you know what it's like to be a child, knowing your own mother turns a blind eye while her lover abuses you?"

Rudra's jaw tightened, but his gun didn't lower. "You could have gone to the police. Why take the law into your own hands?"

Kaali let out a hollow laugh, the sound echoing with bitterness. "The police?" she sneered. "Do you think they're any better? Do you think they wouldn't prey on the children who come to them for help?"

Her words hung heavily in the air, their truth undeniable. But Rudra refused to falter. "Drop the knife," he said firmly, his voice unyielding. "Let the woman go, or I will shoot."

Before Kaali could answer, the air shifted. Durga, who was behind Rudra, raised her arm—and in it, a gun pointed right at his head.

"Durga?" Rudra's voice cracked with incredulity as he shifted a little to the side, his heart sinking. "What's going on?"

"Put down your gun, Rudra," Durga commanded, her voice firm but quivering with something else— something determined.

Rudra's mind was racing, trying to make sense of the betrayal. "Durga, listen to me. You don't have to do this."

Durga's eyes welled with a mix of pain and determination. "You need to let her finish this, Rudra. You don't understand."

"I understand that this isn't justice," Rudra said, his voice softening. "This is revenge."

Durga's hand trembled slightly, her grip on the gun faltering for a moment. But her resolve didn't waver.

Rudra's eyes flitted through flashes of the past as Durga spoke, her voice haunting and laced with the weight of old wounds.

She spoke of her sister, Meera, who had once been nothing but a child, sitting outside a closed bedroom door with her younger sister cradled in her lap. She described the muffled whimpers of their mother inside the room and the cruel men who walked in and out, each one leaving a stain of horror on their lives.

Years passed, and the nightmare only worsened.

The mother, blinded by greed and compulsion, had finally sent Meera into that room—into the clutches of a stranger. But the stranger hadn't emerged unscathed. Meera had, her hands shaking and her dress soaked in the stranger's blood. She had wielded a knife and extracted her own form of justice, leaving behind her mother's betrayal and the man's screams as she carried her sister out of that wretched home. "I know what happened to you both," Rudra said, his voice heavy with empathy. "What happened was wrong—unforgivable. But this path you're on isn't justice, Durga. It's a never-ending cycle of pain."

Kaali's voice cut through like a blade. "It is justice. The only justice."

Rudra's heart stung as he gazed between them— the battered, brutal women who had turned their suffering into retribution. "Please," he said softly, his voice almost a prayer. "Free her. Let me assist you in finding another route."

Kaali's gaze flickered with something—a shadow of doubt, perhaps—but it was gone in an instant. Her fingers on the knife grew taut, and she crept closer to her captive.

And then, a shot cracked the night, as Rudra made sense of what Kaali said - "A mother is the first and most sacred protector of her child. But when a mother falters in her duty—whether swayed by lust, greed, or other desires—the child may be forced to rise, don the mantle of Goddess KAALI, and deliver the justice that the mother failed to uphold." The sound lingered on, chilling, a testimony to violence within those walls.

Epilogue

ool night air hung thick around the police station, its heavy stillness punctuated only by the distant hum of moving vehicles. Constable Ali pushed open the heavy door and stepped out, the overhead light throwing a pale glow on his drawn face. The weight of the day stuck to his step as he walked over to his scooter, parked in the corner of the courtyard under a solitary streetlamp that flickered occasionally. The soft rustle of leaves in the wind accompanied him as he stepped onto the seat, tucked his cap into place, and turned the engine on. The familiar buzz filled the air, momentarily blending with the barking of a dog in the distance. Ali turned out onto the road, taking the quiet lanes easily.

The night had left over the city a sort of subdued calm, but his approach to the market street undermined this stillness. A few vendors were still seen tending to customers at this hour of night at the market. Neon signs flashed above small stalls, throwing down their garish light on the cobbled street. The tangy scent of spices and the faint aroma of grilled meat wafted through the air, mingling with intermittent bursts of laughter from a nearby group of men. Ali slowed his scooter, his eyes sweeping across the lively scene. He brought the vehicle to a stop in front of the butcher's shop, where the fluorescent sign hummed faintly. The shopkeeper, a wiry man with sharp features and an apron smeared with fresh blood, looked up from behind the counter. Ali stepped off his scooter and approached the counter, his voice steady yet informal. "One special," he said, nodding slightly.

The shopkeeper's face broke into a knowing grin. "One special for Ali bhai," he replied, reaching for a fresh cut.

Ali stood beside his scooter, one hand resting casually on the handlebars. His eyes remained alert, scanning the dwindling crowd with the vigilance that came naturally to a man in uniform. Moments later, a boy emerged from the back of the shop, carrying a neatly wrapped parcel. He handed it to Ali with a quick smile. "Here you go, Ali bhai."

Ali nodded in response, securing the package under his arm as he turned to walk away. Without another word, he mounted his scooter, fired up the engine, and faded back into the sparse traffic. The glow of the market faded into the rearview mirror as he rode away, the hum of the scooter melting into the quiet rhythm of the night.

Reaching his neighbourhood, Ali began to feel the familiarity of a low-ceilinged home as a faint sensation of relief. The porch light above illuminated the front gate, but its soft glow was quite attractive as he parked the scooter beside the steps. Then he killed the engine, and there he stood for a while, looking around in an uncomfortable silence. The street had a lonely look, with the window shades of one house fluttering occasionally.

He climbed the stairs and rang the doorbell, the faint chime echoing inside. Within seconds, the door creaked open, and his wife stood in the doorway, her face lit with a quiet smile that spoke of routine and warmth. Ali handed her the meat parcel silently, their exchange needing no words. She took it with a nod and disappeared towards the kitchen as Ali stepped inside.

The faint clatter of dishes came from the dining area as Ali made his way to the bedroom.

The day's fatigue was etched into his movements, but the comforting sounds of home eased some of the tension in his shoulders.

By the time he returned to the dining room, dinner had been served. His wife and teenage son were already seated, their soft murmurs blending with the faint clinking of cutlery on plates. Ali settled back in his chair, the warmth of the food and the familiarity of his family's presence providing a brief respite. Just as he would take his first bite, the shrill ringing of his phone cut through the silence. Ali glanced at the device; its screen glowed with the name of the caller. He sighed, then moved his hand to reach for it as he pushed back his chair.

"Ali speaking," he said, his voice low as he walked towards the window. Far across the city, Rudra sat in his living room, the soft glow of the television illuminating the relaxed faces of his family. Anvi leaned comfortably against him, her laughter ringing out at the comedy show they were watching. Meera sat cross-legged on the floor, her eyes fixed on the screen, her smile warm and unguarded.

The sudden buzz of Rudra's phone broke the moment. He glanced at the caller ID, his expression changing from relaxed to serious in an instant. He rose from the couch and walked to a quieter corner of the room.

"Sir, there's a missing case," the voice on the other end informed him.

Rudra's grip tightened on the phone as the weight of it all settled over him. He turned to Meera, sensing that she had picked up on his change of mood. Her eyes searched him, a silent question. He gave her a nod, brief and laced with a faint smile that seemed to carry with it a sense of reassurance, but which also seemed to hint at something still unresolved. She smiled, small and understanding, and then returned her gaze to the television.

Meanwhile, Ali stood by the window, his gaze drifting toward the dining table. His wife and son continued their meal, unaware of the conversation taking place just a few feet away. Ali's eyes lingered on them, the faintest hint of regret flashing across his face before he refocused on the voice in his ear.

The night seemed darker elsewhere, in a room devoid of warmth or familiarity. It was broken by the cold, clinical hum of a refrigerator when a trolley rolled across the cement floor. Flickers of light overhead cast long shadows on the walls that seemed to dance with the slow and deliberate movements of some figure pushing the trolley.

The figure halted almost exactly in the middle of the room, reaching out to grasp and fling open the refrigerator door with a heavy clanking of its lid. A curl of mist shot forth from within, coiling around the girl lying inside, her face frost-rimmed, her limbs so pale and fragile as the figure delicately lifted her up and laid her on the steel table close by.

Every movement was deliberate, every motion precise. The figure's steady, unflinching hands reached for a great cutting knife that rested on the edge of the table. With a measured motion, the figure tied his hair back, making sure nothing obscured his work. The glint of the blade caught the dim light, reflecting the ominous stillness of the room.

In one swift motion, the blade came down, and the sickening sound of flesh being sliced filled the air. Blood spattered across the figure's face, dark droplets staining the skin. Calmly, almost methodically, the figure wiped his face clean, his movements devoid of urgency or emotion.

As the light shifted slightly, the figure became identifiable. It was Officer Khaleel, his face expressionless, as he stood over the gruesome scene. There was no remorse in his eyes; only a mechanical focus as if he were doing a task. The room fell silent once more, except for the soft hum of the refrigerator and the distant echo of the city's life outside the walls.

About the Author

Vishal Punna is a dynamic and multifaceted personality whose journey spans the worlds of sports, technology, and the arts. A former Davis Cup tennis player from Hyderabad, India, Vishal spent more than three decades playing wonderful tennis, representing his nation with distinction. While he was shaped by sports to be disciplined and resilient, his passionate love for storytelling and creativity stayed with him throughout.

Transitioned from the successful athletic stint, Vishal went for information technology, a completely different field from that where his skills were only developed on the silver screen. Cinema magic again invited him to revisit his artistic fields. He returned to India and ventured into the world of filmmaking. He soon marked his entry as a director with the critically acclaimed short film Jiah - Behind Closed Doors. The film has earned accolades and a prestigious nomination at the Goa International Film

Competition, showing the prowess of Vishal as a storyteller.

Today, Vishal puts his passion for telling stories into words through writing novels. He weaves and pens bright, emotionally intense stories by combining cinematic brilliance with literary depth in every novel he writes. Each page unfolds an unforgettable journey with characters that resonate, emotions lingering, and stories that open up with cinematic brilliance.

...✍